MINDGAMES: FOOL'S MATE

BY

NEAL ASHER

MINDGAMES: FOOL'S MATE

Prologue

With a casual assurance Jason Carroll stooped and shrugged his shoulders forwards so his jacket bulked loose, but the automatic still hung as heavy as an accusation in its shoulder holster, its barrel warm against his chest. He should have dumped it in the river with the silencer, but then he had only dumped that because it was old and needed repacking and he knew where he could get a better one. Anyway, he was not going to panic just because there had been a couple of close calls during the hit. He scrubbed at the spots of blood on his sleeve then looked round the crowded high street. No watchers, no pursuers.

As he stepped from the kerb he knew with smug assurance that he had evaded them. He was better than them, that was all. He had the training. The bus, however , he could neither evade nor avoid, and no amount of training could fend off several tons of diesel accelerated steel. Moreover, he did not even see it. He was facing in the wrong direction. When he heard the rumble of the engine and the squealing of brakes and began to turn he was too late. As it knocked him to the ground and its wheel crushed his chest his last coherent thought in life was, *Oh shit!*

Nothing else seemed appropriate.

There was no pain. His punctured heart beat once or twice pumping salty-warm blood out of his mouth onto the tarmac, and as that one thought occurred to him he knew viscerally that this was it. There would be blackness, nothing. He lay there thinking nothing, readying himself for a state of nothingness, waiting. The next thing he knew he found himself gazing down on the crowd gathering round his body. He recognized two of his pursuers nodding in satisfaction and walking away. They confirmed what he believed: he was dead, yet, no black nothingness had come to engulf him. He found this vaguely disappointing, and now began to entertain nagging doubts.

Is there an afterlife?

He had heard of out-of-the-body experiences and considered them to be merely delusion. In his line of work he had seen and caused quite a lot of death and it had always seemed pretty final, now though, now he was beginning to wonder.

He began to drift upwards, away from his body, which was a relief. He could have gone down. Next, a tunnel of light lay before him and a feeling of extension, as if he were pulling into an infinitely long string, then being wound in far away.

Fisher of men? Oh please not. Not the harps.

It occurred to him that he was not treating his situation with the seriousness it deserved. Perhaps, he surmised, it was the lack of a body and its needs that did that. He became completely detached, merely an awareness.

I exist, I am, was all that he knew for a time.

Chapter One

Gradually, from out of a blank numbness, Carroll became aware of feeling. *I have a body,* he decided, with wonder. Then he wondered if he would find himself in a hospital bed, all his cynicisms proved true and the only people waiting to reel him in being members of Her Majesty's Constabulary. He opened his eyes, then shut them quickly. But closed eyes did not erase the images, and he could certainly fell that he was not lying down.

Did a bus really hit me? Or have I just gone stark staring mad?

He opened his eyes again. Nothing had changed. This particular delusion had distinctly worrying tenacity and, still of logical mind, Carroll decided it would be best to treat it as reality. It would save on confusion.

The men in the other chairs were fighters. This was obvious at a glance. To Carroll's right there sat a Roman legionary. To his left sat a World War One corporal who seemed to have something wrong with his face. And there were more fighting men from the various ages of Earth, seated on wooden chairs on a steel plain that stretched to seeming infinity.

No horizon could be discerned though in one direction the sun seemed to be setting. Carroll stared at it for a moment, is mind blank, then he drew his gaze away and saw that on the other side of the group the plain was paved with hexagons, each one a good twenty feet across. There were seven colours in all and they were arranged so that no two hexagons of the same colour met. They stretched into a distance without horizon.

'All you men are fighters,' said someone from the front of the group. 'This will be plainly evident to those from the later eras, but needed to be stated for those from the younger ages of Earth.'

Carroll jerked as if catching himself drifting off during a briefing then peered past his fellows and saw what appeared to be a Prussian General in full regalia, his moustache waxed perfectly level, marching up and down as he lectured, a swagger stick tucked under his arm. As Carroll watched he realized that the man was not speaking English, but that the words were somehow being translated for him. *Play it cool*, he decided. *Listen to what he has to say then make decisions.* The General continued.

'For this reason alone you have been resurrected,' he said.

Carroll stiffened in shock, no longer cool.

Christ, yes! I was dead!

It had seemed a distant thing until then. He checked those around him and saw that they were reacting similarly. An SS officer leapt to his feet and shouted something, then suddenly others were doing the same. Carroll remained in his seat, taking deep breaths, calming himself.

Take it slowly: listen, learn, act.

'Sit down!' ordered the General, and made a stabbing motion with his swagger stick. All who had been standing were slammed down into their seats. Carroll felt himself pinioned by some force.

'Now,' continued the General, rolling one end of his waxed moustache between his fingertips, 'you will listen to me, and when I have finished, there will be no questions, just obedience.'

'Obey a God damned Prussian! Never!' came a shout.

Carroll glanced aside and saw that this had come from a British Redcoat. Carroll transferred his attention back to the

General to see what his reaction would be. The General stood motionless staring at something beyond the group. Carroll tried to turn his head but found he was unable to. Another member of the group shouted something, then another, and it seemed that cacophony would result, until the General gave his command.

'Be silent!' and he stabbed with his swagger stick.

And they were silent.

'As I was saying,' he continued, 'you have been resurrected because you are fighters, resurrected to take part in the game...' He looked from one face to another. No one said anything; no one was able to.

This is wrong. I am not reacting as I should.

Ephemeral thoughts. All he could do was sit and listen.

'Look there,' said the General, and pointed with his swagger stick. Without volition Carroll turned to look where indicated, as did the rest of the group. He now saw where the plain was paved with that patchwork of coloured hexagons.

'That is where the game takes place,' the General continued. 'The rules, so far as you men are concerned, are simply that you occupy the hexagons indicated to you by the colour of the light set in your wrist-band...' Carroll knew what was coming. *Like chess,* he thought. He wondered how this was being translated to the Roman, to the Turag, and to those others of races and from ages he did not know. '...should you encounter anyone in the hexagon you are moved to you must kill them with the weapons provided. Further instructions will be communicated to you via the translator communicators in your ears.' He paused and Carroll found the restraint on his head released. He turned to face forwards. The General stood before them with his arms akimbo and his expression grim. 'Disobedience is punishable by the offender being burnt to death.'

I am in Hell, thought Carroll.

The General continued relentlessly, 'And it would be well for you to all remember that no punishment here is final. Immediately after punishment the offender will be resurrected to take his place in the game.'

I am definitely in Hell...

'Now, one last thing. You are a team, and there are three other teams.' He pointed directly across the game-board. 'Across there is Anubis's team. To the right is Kali's team, and to the left is the team of Quetzalcoatl, the Feathered Serpent. You men are the Reaper's team.'

So I am in Hell and doomed to fight or burn. I shall fight.

'A number and a colour will now appear on your wrist bands, this directs you to your starting hexagons. Take your positions.'

Carroll felt all hold on him released. He stood and swayed and knew in an instant that in some way his emotions had been suppressed. He peered at his wrist. On it he wore a chrome band with no discernible joint. It had a square glass set in it like a watch face. This glass was red and had on it the number four. Carroll checked towards the game-board then back towards the General, who seemed expectant as he surveyed the group intently. Carroll wondered how he would fare if he attacked the man now, at the start. Before he could come to a decision the SS officer yelled and dived towards the General.

He never made it.

A flash of red light knocked the officer out of the air. He hit the steel screaming and writhing as flame and oily smoke gusted about him in the spastic thrashing of his limbs. Shortly his movements slowed and his screams turned to gurgles. On his hands and knees he shook himself like a dog then collapsed, a blackened atomy, with pink and oozing flesh showing through its many splits and cracks.

This was what the General was waiting for.

And as Carroll realized this he felt the last mental restraint fall from him. He stopped himself from retching as emotion started to fill out the skeletal functioning of his mind. He saw that others had been unable to. The General had not changed his position in the slightest. He just stood there with a wry smile on his face, slowly twisting his moustache between his fingertips. After a moment he stopped this and gazed at something behind them all.

'That was the object lesson,' he said, 'one that never fails to impress. Now you may turn and face your master.'

Carroll turned, something he had not even thought to do a moment earlier. He realized that this had all been perfectly choreographed to bring them to an understanding of the reality of their situation. He turned, and felt his mouth go dry.

Slightly to the right, and a short distance away, stood a blocky flat-topped mirror glass building. To the left stood a machine vaguely like rocket engine ripped out of a Saturn Five then inset with a door. Carroll hardly noticed them. His attention fixed on the massive throne directly in front of them, and the cowled figure seated upon it. The figure's skull face was only half hidden in shadow, and in its right, skeletal hand, it held an enormous scythe. Here then, was the Grim Reaper. Carroll watched as it deposited a small red disk into a box set in the arm of its throne. It then regarded them all with hollow eye sockets, before with a rattle of bony knuckles it gestured to the strangely-shaped machine. The thick fridge-like door of the machine thumped open with a gout of vapour to spill the naked form of the SS officer, his expression haunted and half mad.

'Take your positions,' whispered the Reaper, its deathly voice penetrating the silence like a stiletto. They did as instructed.

♠♠♠

Red four, thought Carroll as he moved to the edge of the game-board. Shortly he found his place and stepped onto it, his shoes clicking on the glassy surface. To his right was green five, quickly occupied by a World War II GI. Brown three, to his left, remained unoccupied.

The GI was a heavily built man with cropped red hair and thick features. Dressed in an American army-issue flack-jacket, camouflage trousers, black boots and a helmet he seemed the archetypal yank, down to the half-smoked Havana clamped in the corner of his mouth.

'Jesus Christ!' he said, then, 'Name's David Ellery. What's yours?'

'Jason Carroll,' He tried not to laugh at this rote politeness, since he felt his laughter might not sound too healthy. About to continue he paused, noticing something odd with Ellery's face.

Like the corporal.

In set along his jawbone was a grid half an inch by an inch. Carroll was about to ask about that, but then reached up and touched his own jawbone. He had one as well.

'What is that?' asked the GI.

'You should know as well as I,' said Carroll. Ellery reached up and touched the grid set in his jaw and panic twisted his features. Carroll continued, 'No doubt to complement the translators in our ears.' He glanced around and saw that all the fighters whose faces he could see had one of these inset grids.

'Tell me, Carroll, did you die?' Ellery abruptly asked, the question almost a plea.

Carroll pretended to consider the question as he fingered the grid and dragged his thoughts to order, then replied, 'Yes.' He distinctly remembered the taste of heart's blood in his mouth. 'You also, I presume?'

Ellery was reluctant. 'Yeah... well, I think so. It happened pretty quickly... grenade.'

'Do you believe in Hell?' asked Carroll.

'No way bud, there has to be a reason for this...'

'Yes, presumably there has to be,' said Carroll, turning away.

'You going to fight, Carroll?'

Carroll turned and gazed back towards the Reaper. Nearby the SS officer was putting on a new uniform he had been given. A short distance from him lay his still-smoking primary corpse.

'There was not one moment of spontaneity during that briefing. Our friend there was probably primed to act the way he did, even though it might have been against his will. They do not want robots I think, but I wonder what rules there are to limit how they may tamper with us...' He touched the grid again then studied Ellery. The GI was peering at him in confusion. Carroll gestured to the SS officer. 'Yes, I shall fight.'

Ellery peered uncertainly in the same direction, then he grinned wryly. 'Yeah, guess I'll fight as well. Sure gave that bastard a taste of his own medicine though.'

Carroll nodded, half to Ellery but mostly to himself as he mentally recited his litany, *listen, learn, act.*

'It seems to me,' he said after a moment, 'that we were brought here the moment we died, but not immediately resurrected.'

'Yeah, that's what I thought. Looks like a military history pageant, but where is here?'

Carroll regarded the twilight sky. There were stars but no recognizable constellations.

'Not on Earth.'

Ellery peered up also. 'I guess not.' Then again studying Carroll asked, 'When did you die?'

'Nineteen eighty-four,' said Carroll.

'Eighty-four! Hell! I could be your granddad!'

'No, I think not. I am strictly British. By the way, Hitler's Germany lost.'

'That was going to be my next question,' said Ellery wryly. 'When did it end? I got snuffed in forty-four.'

'You missed it by a year.'

'Hell! ... Ah well, I guess it's good to know we won. By the way, what are you? You look like a banker.'

Carroll peered down at his grey suit. It was the same as the one he had been wearing when the bus had run over him, only this suit did not conceal a silenced automatic. That had been one of the first things he had checked.

'Special Air Service,' he stated flatly, aware that Ellery had probably never heard of it, 'for a while, then I did a little freelance work.'

'Mercenary?'

'Sometimes...'

'So I guess you got yours the same way as I did?'

'More or less,' said Carroll, feeling slightly embarrassed.

Ellery gave him a probing look then turned away to check his surroundings. After a moment he turned back, finding words to try and hold back the reality of their situation.

'Come on, how? How did you...'

'I got run over by a bus,' said Carroll succinctly.

Ellery burst out laughing, his laughter holding that hysterical edge Carroll feared his own might have held had he allowed himself laughter. Carroll waited patiently for him to finish before continuing, 'You see, I was too good to end up getting killed by an enemy soldier, or agent, so it had to be something like that, or old age.' It then occurred to him that the bus driver had not blown his horn, and when he had seen himself dying there had been no bus visible. Ellery eyed him uncertainly, not sure what to make of him.

Shortly brown three was occupied by the SS officer, dressed in a new and perfectly-pressed black uniform. He was subdued, frightened, and Carroll almost felt sorry for him … almost.

'You lost the war!' Ellery shouted over at him.

'I am aware of that,' said the officer, the voice Carroll heard bearing no relation to the movement of his lips and confirming Carroll's thought about the purpose of the grids, 'I was stabbed to death by a Jewess at the Nuremberg trials.'

Ellery looked askance at Carroll, who gave him a short but concise explanation of said trials.

'Ha! So much for the Thousand Year Reich and the Aryan super race.'

The SS officer just stared at Ellery, his red-rimmed eyes showing starkly in a face that seemed paler than normal because of its contrast with his black uniform. He was another archetype: the blond-haired Aryan German officer. Carroll studied him for a moment and realized he was inspecting the nearest thing known to an evil man. It occurred to him that if this was Hell then no one deserved it more than this man. Yet, in the deterministic world they had come from, he was blameless. Carroll, perhaps, was more evil in his killing for money. But of course this was all idle speculation. Carroll believed in evil as much as he believed life after death...

He turned away, and while doing so saw that the colour on his wristband had changed and that the number had disappeared. He held his wrist up to Ellery and the GI glanced at his own.

'Only you,' he said, 'and if you don't move you end up feeling like the Thanksgiving turkey.' Carroll nodded, smiled grimly, and then he stepped to the only blue hexagon that butted against his own.

'Hey, Carroll, what do you reckon the range is of that thing Rommel here got zapped with?' Ellery asked.

'You're assuming it is a single weapon?'

'What else?'

'Perhaps our bodies have some kind of explosive device fitted, radio activated. I don't suppose these are our original bodies, and Rommel's certainly isn't.'

'The name is Kruger,' said the SS officer.

'Kruger,' repeated Carroll. 'What was it like, Kruger?'

'To be burnt to death?' said Kruger with a faint sneer.

'No, to be resurrected,' said Carroll.

Kruger grinned nastily. 'Perhaps you will be finding out soon,' he said.

Carroll glanced towards Ellery with his expression grim.

Ellery pursed his lips then shrugged, after a moment he too inspected his wristband.

'My turn,' he said with forced levity.

'Join the charge,' said Carroll with bitter irony, then he checked from side to side and saw that others were advancing also. Soon he was moved forwards again, then again, the delays between each move getting shorter and shorter as the pace of the game picked up. In very little time his starting hexagon was out of sight. Ellery had moved some way in front of him and to the right, and Kruger behind him and to the left. They were closer to each other than to anyone else in the team, and as they advanced across the surreal plain they made a very odd trio indeed: the American GI, lauded as a hero by his friends, the SS officer, and the hit man. Carroll managed to dismiss the oddity of the situation and focus on immediate reality of killing and dying, no matter how temporary that death might be. After a time he saw the first of the opposition. The man was quite obviously and ancient Egyptian and he was drawing closer and closer to Ellery.

'What the Hell are we doing here?!' shouted Ellery from his hexagon. Good question, one that it seemed pointless to ask at this point.

Carroll shouted, 'Playing games!' His heart began to thump heavily, and he began to feel a deep fear of imminent physical pain laced with a numbing confusion. What the Hell was going on? *Stay cool. Stay cool. What is this? Delayed reaction?* He scanned his surroundings as if for the first time. Suddenly he needed a cigarette and wondered crazily how this body could be addicted to nicotine

'Go to it, Ellery!' Carroll shouted across at the GI as the Egyptian moved in.

Ellery saluted to him then stepped into a green hexagon at the same time as the Egyptian. There was a scramble for something in the middle of the hexagon, then Ellery and his opponent stepped away from each other. Each of them held a long handled mace. They circled. Ellery feinted to the left then pulled back to swing from the right, and it was all over. Ellery stumbled. The Egyptian moved in close and brought his mace down on Ellery's head. Even Carroll heard the crunch, and in a moment, saw the red liquid pooling round the GI's prostrate form. It seemed to Carroll as if it must be paint, then the pragmatic side of his nature asserted itself and he knew that it was not. The Egyptian dropped his club and moved to the next hexagon, and behind him Ellery's corpse became a sudden bonfire.

Carroll felt sick and angry. He turned away, and in doing so, noted that there were other fires burning across the plain. Mechanically he moved to the next hexagon indicated, noting it started him on a path towards the Egyptian.

They met on a green hexagon. As soon as they stepped onto it candent flash ignited at the centre and, then faded to reveal two poniards. So this is the way, thought Carroll. He stepped forwards and snatched up the poniard nearest him then leapt back. He bowed mockingly towards the Egyptian.

'My name is Jason Carroll,' he said.

The Egyptian stared at him blankly for a moment then saluted.

'I am Ramses, the second of that name,' he said, and threw his poniard.

For a moment there was no pain, just blank shock at what had happened; such an easy and deadly trick. Carroll peered down at the handle of the poniard where it protruded from his chest. Distractedly he observed the frothy arterial blood pulsing out around it.

Then came the pain.

Every muscle in his body seemed to lock up, and he did not want to move because of the possibility of increasing this agony. He felt sick, dizzy, and fast approached that drunken state before blackout. Once, he had taken a bullet in the leg, but there had been drugs almost immediately. The pain did not compare. His surroundings seemed to dilate, blackness filled the edges of his vision. He fell. The last stutterings of his heart were

15

a drumbeat in his head and again he tasted that salty warm gush in his mouth.

Then he died. Again.

Chapter Two

Walking across the steel plain the Clown drew closer and closer to Carroll. When the clown-face finally loomed over him, it was so much sadder than a clown-face should be, and also more menacing. Frozen, a cold pain in his chest locking him to the spot, Carroll felt an awareness of geologic time... The clown-face tilted, as if preparing to speak. Carroll knew something was wanted of him but felt only terror. Then a gong sounded, and the clown-face shimmered, cracked, fragmented.

A machine-oil smell filled his nostrils, and the taste in his mouth was of a rusty blade wiped across his tongue. Behind his eyes points of light danced like the sun-caught extremities of some deep-sea polyp. Slowly he became aware that he was enclosed. He opened his eyes to darkness and the lights behind his eyes faded to nonexistence. *Where am I?* He wondered. With a thump a line of light appeared to one side of him, then the door to the resurrection machine opened. Belatedly, memory returned as he stumbled out onto the steel plain.

'Ain't that Egyptian somethin',' remarked Ellery. Carroll did not reply as he inspected his naked body. There were no wounds. There were no scars.

'You want clothes? There's another machine in there,' said Ellery, a note of desperation in his voice. Carroll looked up and saw that Eller was clad in the same kind of clothing as previously. He even had another half-smoked cigar jammed in the corner of his mouth. He was attempting to appear nonchalant, but without much success.

'Show me,' Carroll said.

Ellery led him from the resurrection machine across to the mirror-glass building. As he followed, with his bare feet slapping against the metal, Carroll glanced across and saw that the General and the Reaper were motionless, at the edge of the game-board, like toy sentinels. *Could I escape?* He wondered. Then he gazed around at the steel plain stretching to infinity in every direction and wondered where he would escape to. Shaking his head he followed Ellery through the silently opening doors of the mirrored building. As he stepped through the disturbing image of a clown came to the forefront of his mind. He shook, irritated by the image. It was a recurring dream he had suffered after a visit to the circus with his father – a dream that seemed to typify all lost innocence.

Beyond the doors lay a plain boxlike room from which corridors led into the rest of the building. From these Carroll could hear anxious talk, the mournful wail of some musical instrument, and smell food and aromatic or narcotic smokes. The room was cluttered with tables and chairs of light almost cheapish manufacture. Ellery led him to one side where one wall was taken up by pedestal mounted foot-high metal cylinders before which, at waist height, protruded keyboards.

'Over here,' said Ellery, pointing to one cylinder with Carroll's name printed across it in silvered letters. 'This is your one. You just type in what you want and it appears in the booth.'

Carroll reached forwards and typed in 'combat clothing'. On one side of the cylinder a red light flashed a couple of times then went off. The door on the front of the cylinder swung open to reveal neatly folded SAS battledress and a pair of well-polished boots. He dropped the boots on the floor and wondered what he would get if he asked for ruby slippers, but after taking out the clothing instead selected 'underwear' then he began to dress. As he did so he tried to ignore the phantom pain in his chest. It had been the same with the bullet in his leg for many years after.

'How did you learn about this?' he asked Ellery.

'The General,' Ellery replied. 'He told us casualties are always pretty rapid with new recruits. I was the first in. He told me to show the set-up here to everyone who comes in.' He finished with a cracked laugh.

'I see,' said Carroll, then glanced in annoyance across at one of the room's grey walls where for a moment he thought he had seen the painted face of a clown. Ellery was not the only one cracking under the pressure, he decided, and sat down on one of the chairs to tie his boots.

'What is this, Carroll?' Ellery asked, obviously still on edge.

Carroll glanced up to see that all Ellery's pretence at nonchalance had gone. He appeared ill. The cigar was out of his mouth and held tightly in his shaking hand.

'Calm down,' said Carroll, because he had no answers and wondering if there was any answer they could comprehend. Ellery stared at him blankly for a moment then shook his head as if coming out of a trance.

'Yeah, what I need is a drink.' He stepped to the booth with his name printed on it, tapped something out, and in a moment returned with a bottle of Jack Daniels and two glasses. He sat down on the other side of the table from Carroll and poured out whisky. Carroll took the glass proffered, but did not gulp the contents like Ellery.

'I suppose,' said Carroll, between careful sips of the spirit, 'that what we have to do is simply consider ourselves in

19

enemy territory. We're doing a recon.' He carefully placed the glass down on the table between his elbows and interlaced his fingers before his face. 'What we have to do is watch, listen, learn, then see what we can do about our situation. Let's collate the information we have so far... no matter how strange it might seem. Our situation could not be much stranger than it is.'

His approach had a calming effect on Ellery, or perhaps it was the drink, another glass of which the GI poured before replying.

'We're in a game,' he said.

'Precisely,' said Carroll, without a trace of mockery in his voice, then went on with, 'There are four... creatures who are resurrecting fighters for some kind of board game. Our creature has the powers of life and death over us... and other powers.'

'The power to give orders that have to be obeyed,' began Ellery, 'the General–'

'Yes,' interrupted Carroll, then took a sip of his whisky before going on, 'his swagger stick.'

'What?' said Ellery, choking on his drink.'

'Baton,' Carroll translated.

Ellery went on, 'Yeah, each time he gave an order he waved it about and made the order... stick.'

'Precisely,' said Carroll. 'What else do we have?'

Ellery looked thoughtful for a moment then said, 'The red disc–' but Carroll interrupted again.

'You saw, good. When Kruger burnt the Reaper was holding up a disc. Afterwards he dropped it into a box on the arm of his throne. It sounded as if there were more discs in that box.'

Ellery gazed at him with annoyance then asked, 'You think there's a connection – one disc for each of us?'

'Perceptive,' Carroll nodded his head and smiled perfunctorily. Ellery appeared more annoyed than ever as Carroll went on, 'The discs and the baton, they are the greatest danger to us.' His tone was that of a school master lecturing a particularly thick child.

'Smug bastard ain't you,' said Ellery, obviously unable to stand Carroll's attitude any longer.

Carroll leant back in his chair, gulped down his drink, then propped his boots up on another chair.

'Practical psychology old chap,' he said with straight-faced precision. Ellery stared at him for a time, seeming at one point as if he was about to throw a punch. Then he turned away trying to hide a grin that had come unbidden to his face. When he finally got control of himself he turned back, straight-faced.

'Limey turd,' he said succinctly.

'GI arsehole,' Carroll replied, and simultaneously they burst out laughing. From then, until ten minutes later when the door of the resurrection machine thumped open, they forgot what lay beyond their laughter.

♠♠♠

Kruger was the next person from the resurrection machine, followed, even as Carroll and Ellery exited the building, by a tall kinky-haired African with skin as black as ebony. Ellery ignored Kruger and introduced himself to the African. Kruger tagged along behind when Ellery led the way back inside. Carroll just observed.

The African did not speak English, but with the translator device this was no hindrance to communication. It was his attitude that was a hindrance. Under Ellery's instruction he learnt how to operate his creation booth. All he gave in return

21

was his name, or rather a translation of his name, Stridefar, and once dressed in his red robe, strode proudly to the door then outside.

Ellery shrugged then turned to Carroll, 'What does he think he is?'

'Masai,' said Kruger from where he now stood by his own creation booth, struggling into his black uniform, 'a south Kenyan race... mixed Hamitic stock.'

Ellery whirled on him, 'Of course you'd know all about races wouldn't you?'

Kruger glared at him, hate evident in every nuance of his stance. Carroll turned away and sat down. Infighting like this did not interest him, and he wanted to make this obvious to Ellery. Ellery glanced round at him, back at Kruger, then after a moment re-joined him at the table.

'I think there a plenty of enemies here for us already,' Carroll said scathingly.

Ellery appeared sheepish. They both now turned to watch Kruger who was dressed now, and operating his creation machine. Shortly he took a piece of paper from the booth, screwed it up in disgust and threw it away. Then he typed in something else. This time he got what he had requested: a bottle of schnapps and a tumbler. These he took to the table furthest from Ellery and Carroll.

'Probably asked for a Luger or a stick grenade,' stated Ellery, then took out a piece of paper similar to the one Kruger had screwed up and handed it to Carroll. It had 'request denied' printed on it.

'I tried for some grenades.'

'You're aware of how effective they are then?' asked Carroll with a grin.

'Ain't it the truth,' replied Ellery, grinning also.

22

♠♠♠

In the hours that followed more and more members of the Reaper's team came through the resurrection machine. Ellery, now becoming a little unsteady on his feet, delegated the task of demonstrating the creation booths to a Roman legionary. Together he and Carroll got steadily drunker. Sometime later, when the steadiness had gone out of their drinking and they were sharing the last dregs of the bottle, a gong sounded.

I know that sound, thought Carroll, and as he stared into his whisky glass he saw the sad sad face of a clown, broken up by the light reflecting ripples of the liquor.

'That means somethin',' slurred Ellery.

'Sure does,' Carroll slurred back, and carefully moved his glass to one side before allowing his head to thud down on the surface of the table.

'By the soul-sound of the Clown, Anubis is declared the winner,' announced the General from the door. There was more, but by then Carroll had slumped into whisky-sodden slumber.

Chapter Three

The Clown cried out for freedom, sandwiched between earth and low sky both the colour of dull rubies. He ran to the unseen horizon, white greasepaint melting from the anger and sorrow of his face.

Like a receding projectile the image shrank and grew distant, became a disc, falling, with other discs, from a skeletal hand. In the other discs, held in two-dimensional traps were Ellery, Kruger, the legionary, the Masai. Even in sleep Carroll knew that someone, somewhere, was trying to tell him something. As he sank finally into sleep beyond dreams he had a momentary understanding of the perfection of certain shapes, and fleeting vision of an immense disc with a sun at its centre.

There was a foul taste in his mouth and a blacksmith was making horseshoes in his head. He opened his eyes to find himself in a small white-walled room sprawled on an oval sleeping platform that had been folded down from the wall. The room reverberated with the sound of snoring and he glanced across it to see Ellery laid out on a similar platform. He ignored the GI and continued to study the room. For a moment he could not figure out what was wrong with it, then he realised that it was hexagonal. He sat upright and swung his legs off of the platform, the throbbing of his head growing worse. He needed a pint of water and aspirin he decided. He scanned around for the source of these essentials.

The walls of the room were scattered with hexagonal cupboard doors. He stood and walked unsteadily to one of these and opened it. Nothing but dusty shelves. He tried them all and all were empty but one. The one held a pair of petrified leather sandals. He wondered when the room had last been occupied and what had happened to those occupants.

On opposing sides of the room were doors shaped like squashed hexagons, which slid aside when he approached. The first one led out into a corridor lined with many more doors like it. The second opened into this place's equivalent of a bathroom. A circular indentation in the floor, three feet by three feet, sat below an oversized shower head. To one side stood something like a urinal you could sit on, and all around the edges of the room were deep troughs above which ran ribbed water pipes like metal vines. Carroll stepped inside and availed himself of the facilities, and when he returned to the bedroom he felt almost human.

'A positively wonderful morning,' he said to Ellery maliciously. There was a groan from Ellery's bunk followed by a sticky sucking sound as the GI discovered something unpleasant in his mouth.

'Is it ever morning here,' Ellery finally rasped, 'Jesus! My head.'

Carroll   chuckled. 'Whadda you so happy about, Bud? It was me that carried you here after that drunk. Christ! You started slow but you soon caught up. You should be worse than me!' Ellery snapped.

On a serious note Carroll asked, 'Did the General tell you about these rooms?'

'Yeah,' said Ellery bluntly. Carroll chuckled again. Ellery stared at him with bloodshot eyes. 'I bet you're one of those bastards that sing in the mornings as well.'

'A few pints of water to drink and a cold shower does wonders. All I need now is a cup of tea.'

'Yuk,' said Ellery.

Chuckling still, Carroll exited the room. After a short exploration he found the main area with the personalised creation booths. The only other occupant here was the Roman Legionary. He nodded to that one, went to his booth, and typed out for a pot of tea, cup, and jug of milk, and a breakfast of bacon, fried eggs, tomatoes, mushrooms, sausages and bread. His situation might be weird and somewhat deadly, but he was not one to miss out on its advantages. He set this breakfast down on a table, then went to the door. Still sunset out there; forever twilight. However, neither the General nor the Reaper was in sight. What business were they about, he wondered, as he returned to his breakfast.

As he tucked into his food Carroll wondered again about the possibilities of escape. Putting aside the fact that he had no idea of where he would be escaping to, he considered how an escape could be engineered. Quite simply, the Reaper and the General would have to be eliminated and both at the same time as both of them had weapons that could be brought to bear rapidly: the General his baton, and the Reaper those discs. Some co-ordinated action would be necessary so Carroll could not do it by himself. Considering that, he looked up as Ellery entered the room, got himself a pot of coffee, and came to the table.

'Ah, you are still alive then?' he said to the GI.

Ellery gazed at him blearily and did not reply until with a shaking hand and deep concentration he had poured himself a cup of coffee and taken a sip.

'Depends on what you mean by alive,' he said acerbically.

26

Carroll grinned, finished the last of his breakfast then poured himself a cup of tea.

'May I join you?' said the legionary, who had silently approached their table. He was a big, dark-haired man with a square jaw that was cleanly-shaven, unlike Ellery's. His eyes were an incongruous blue, his musculature sharply defined, and his nose inevitably patrician. He wore a white toga with a pattern of laurel leaves embroidered on it, and sandals much like the ones Carroll had found in the cupboard in their room. Carroll liked the look of him; he seemed in control, efficient.

'If you like, yes,' he replied.

The legionary sat down and regarded Ellery with a raised eyebrow before turning back to Carroll.

'I am Julius Daeus Augustus,' he said, and Carroll was interested to note that just for his name the movements of his lips meshed with his translated words. *I'm getting used to it,* he thought. He was becoming inured to strangeness.

'Jason Carroll,' he said, and gesturing to Ellery, 'and this object is David Ellery.'

Ellery nodded once in Julius's direction then leant back in his chair with his eyes closed. The corner of Julius's mouth twisted as he suppressed a grin.

'Ellery doesn't feel well,' said Carroll.

'Yes, so I see,' said Julius. 'I had expected you to be as he is. He walked out of here. You did not.'

Carroll pushed his plate away, leant back, and took out a cigarette. 'I recover quickly,' he said.

Julius did not reply. He was staring in open curiosity as Carroll lit his cigarette.

'I don't suppose you had anything like this in your time?'

Julius frowned in puzzlement.

27

'Time?' he said, then, after shaking his head, 'Certain primitive peoples inhaled the smokes from the leaves of certain plants. They had the same effect as strong wine.'

'This isn't quite the same.'

Julius continued to stare, then after a moment asked, 'May I try one?'

Carroll shook a cigarette from the box and offered it.

'I don't suppose you'll get lung cancer here. I warn you though. You won't like this,' he said.

Julius took the cigarette and held it in his hand like Carroll held his.

'The device you used. May I use it?'

Carroll took out the zippo Ellery had obtained while they were drinking, demonstrated it, then handed it over. Julius lit the cigarette, gazing with fascination at the lighter all the while, then he had a fit of coughing, and with his eyes watering he handed the lighter back.

'You are right. I do not like this. Perhaps I will like the effect though.' Stubbornly he continued to draw on the cigarette.

Their conversation lapsed for a while then as Julius and Carroll smoked and Ellery clutched at his head self-pityingly every time the Roman coughed.

'This place looked like a bomb hit last night,' Carroll eventually commented, 'yes, I suppose you could call it last night. Who cleared up?'

'Before I answer that,' said Julius, 'what is a bomb?'

Carroll studied him for a long moment. 'That did not translate?'

'The machine that speaks for you was silent.'

Carroll nodded, 'A bomb is a weapon that causes great destruction ... like Greek fire.'

Julius nodded, then ruefully studying the end of his cigarette said, 'I know Greek fire.'

Now directing his question wholly at Julius he asked, 'Who cleared up?'

'It was just after he carried you away,' said Julius, gesturing at Ellery. Even the translation showed ironic humour. 'The General kept four of us back to clear away the mess. Everything went into a cylinder through there,' he gestured to one of the doors, 'and disappeared.'

'Mmmm, I suppose it's logical that if they can create things as easily as they do they can destroy things easily as well.'

'Like us,' said Ellery morosely.

Julius and Carroll nodded grim agreement.

The other members of the team soon began to file in: a World War One Tommy, a Cavalier and Roundhead who kept pointedly separate, the Masai, a Turag, four others of some Eastern race Carroll did not recognise, the Redcoat, one who could only have been a Samurai, and of course, Kruger. They all settled down in their various groups and began eating, drinking, and speaking in their various translated and untranslated languages. Shortly after they were all gathered the General came in from outside to be met by an abrupt silence.

'You have all rested and eaten,' he said, and took out a large pocket watch, which immediately reminded Carroll of a certain white rabbit created by a namesake of his. 'The game will commence in one half of an hour,' he finished, then turned and left. Carroll wondered how his words had come out to the others. He turned to Ellery.

'It's strange that we all understand what he is saying,' he said. Ellery peered at him dimly. Carroll continued, 'What does 'one half of an hour' translate as to people who have never known clocks?'

Ellery glanced pointedly at Julius.

Julius said, 'I know what a clock is ... I understood him.'

He sounded amazed at his own perceptiveness.

'You know what that means don't you?' Carroll said grimly to them both.

Julius seemed completely lost, whilst Ellery's face bore a pained expression, which only gradually cleared. He then nodded in grim agreement.

'I do not understand,' said Julius.

Carroll explained, 'It means that our minds have been tampered with.'

'What else do you reckon they've done?' asked Ellery.

Carroll shrugged, 'Placed inhibitions. Taken away our urge to escape or weakened it. Cut down on our panic reactions. When you think about it, our behaviour has been pretty subdued considering our situation here.'

'I have noticed this,' said Julius, 'I do not think of gods... yet I... I am sure that... I mean, I died?'

'You died,' Carroll affirmed.

'Yes,' said Julius, bowing his head and staring at the table top, 'I know of few who have survived a sword in the stomach.'

Overcome by curiosity Ellery asked, 'Who did that to you?'

'One of the islanders of Nothern Britain, a mad race, completely uncontrollable.'

Something concerning a story he had once heard occurred to Carroll then.

'What legion were you in?'

'The Ninth.'

Carroll nodded to himself. 'I know ... knew, historians who would have a lot to ask you.'

Julius glanced up from the table top. 'Historians?!' he repeated with something approaching panic, and swung his attention from Carroll to Ellery then back again.

Carroll regarded him speculatively. How much had his mind been fooled with?

'You are not fully aware of the situation then?' then after a pause, 'to me and Ellery the Roman Empire is history, like, a couple of thousand years in our past.'

Julius gaped at him, before finally managing,' 'I thought your dress was strange, but the Empire is large.' He stared at the table top again.

Carroll nodded. 'All the people here are from different ages.'

'What ... what happened to the Empire?'

'It decayed,' replied Carroll, then stood up. 'Let's go outside.'

Julius and Ellery stood and followed him.

The Reaper and the General were still as statues, facing each other as if conferring, but preternaturally silent.

'Empires fall and rise, ages pass. As human beings we must face the trials of the moment,' said Carroll pointedly. The three silently regarded their foe.

After a time the General turned from the Reaper and gazed across at them. Then, after pressing his finger against his ear he turned to face the building.

'The game is shortly to commence. Muster immediately.' The instruction came through Carroll's translator as if the man was standing right next to him. He glanced round at Ellery and Julius who both signified that they had heard the instruction as well.

♠♠♠

Shortly the fighters began to file out of the building and approach the General. They came reluctantly, but they came. The General watched them with his monocled eye like some scientist studying mediocre specimens. When they were all seated in the chairs he turned once again to the Reaper. It was then that Kruger suddenly stood up and approached them. A muttered conversation ensued. The General nodded, and Kruger resumed his seat. As he did so the Reaper swung towards the building. An interval of stillness and silence was broken by a sudden low but powerful AC hum issuing from the Reaper's throne. With sinister deliberation the Reaper turned its skeletal head to stare out across the steel plain. Abruptly the hum became a roar and the throne howled into the air to hover about thirty feet from the ground.

Shielding his eyes from the sudden gusting and swirling of the wind Carroll watched as the throne rotated until it wavered on then centres on one direction like a compass needle. The Reaper then reached into the arm of its throne and removed a disc. A glare of ruby light ignited between the Reaper's eye socket and the disc. Distantly Carroll thought he heard a scream, though that could have been his imagination since it was obvious what was happening. The light flashed out of existence, the Reaper replaced the disc in the box, and the throne began to settle with the winding down roar of a jet turbine. Carroll now watched the resurrection machine. The door thumped open, and out staggered the Cavalier. He had tried to escape and failed.

The General broke the silence, speaking as if nothing of consequence had happened. But then death seemed to have no consequence in this place.

'The rules of the game are now more complex,' he said, twirling the end of a moustache between his fingertips, 'as before, you will move to the hexagons you are directed to, and as before you will fight to the death anyone you find there. These basic rules remain the same.' No one spoke. All watched and waited. The General continued, 'However, you will receive additional vocal instructions, sometimes telling you to follow light lines that will appear on the ground, telling you what to do with some weapons, and occasionally telling you to defend more than one hexagon. This will all come clear to you during the game. Now, take your positions.'

The General finished his speech with a wave of his baton. Carroll looked askance at Ellery then walked to blue five as his wristband instructed him.

♠♠♠

The game commenced as it had before. Carroll went to his starting hexagon and Kruger and Ellery moved into positions either side of him. Shortly he was moved to the next hexagon in, then the next and the next. It was after he stepped into the seventh hexagon that things began to change.

'Follow the yellow line,' came the General's curt instruction in his ear. He peered down at a yellow line that had appeared, growing from where he stood and extending itself into the next hexagon at a walking pace. He followed where it directed him, knowing it would certainly not be back to Kansas.

As he entered the next hexagon the line began to grow at a greater rate. He glanced back and saw that it was now shrinking from behind and was already out of the hexagon he had started in. He picked up his pace to keep with the line. It did not take much imagination to guess what would happen if he did not.

To begin with he was trotting to keep up, then finally, running. All his concentration centred on getting his breath and following the line. Then, it came to a halt, and gasping, he halted with it. As it faded he cursed himself for smoking. After all, his new body was probably free of addiction. Once he had his breath back he checked his wristband to confirm that he was in the correct hexagon, then stood upright and scanned around.

Scattered all around there were combatants swinging at each other with clubs, knives, and other weapons of death. There were others sprinting to keep up with lines, and still others, like Carroll, who were waiting their turn. Amongst all this were ubiquitous oily balefires that told of both victory and defeat. Directly ahead of him Carroll saw three possible opponents advancing on him a hexagon at a time. They appeared to be ancient Egyptians so he guessed they were from Anubis's team. To one side he saw the recently resurrected Cavalier, advancing a hexagon at a time to intercept the three. Carroll watched as he entered a hexagon at the same time as one of the three, the ensuing rush to grab weapons, then the two backing off clutching sabres. Next they quickly engaged, and the Egyptian did not stand a chance. He was decapitated in seconds.

'General instruction,' the General informed his team. Carroll would have laughed at the pun at any other time and in any other place. 'Retain your weapons. I repeat: retain your weapons.'

Still grasping his sabre the Cavalier advanced to meet the next Egyptian. Carroll did not see what happened next because a flare of light distracted him. He turned to see a short, broad-bladed sword lying at the centre of his hexagon. He lurched over to grab it up. By the time he turned back to see what had happened to the Cavalier he was dead and burning and the Egyptians were close. One of them, he saw, carried a trident, the other, a morning star, and not the pretty kind.

'Move at will within the red line,' was the General's next instruction. Carroll checked around as a red like appeared to enclose four hexagons including his own. The General continued with, 'Kill all opponents who cross the line. Members of your own team can join you to help with the defence. Do not kill them.'

Somewhat superfluous instructions Carroll thought. He had known what he had to do from the moment the red line had appeared. He checked to see if anyone was being sent to help him. Distantly he could see Julius and closer the Masai, both were coming towards him a hexagon at a time. Having not yet gained a full understanding of the game he did not know if they would reach him before the Egyptians nor if they were being sent to help at all. He turned to face his prospective opponents, wondering if he would ever understand the rules, wondering if there were any.

Judging the pace at which they were approaching Carroll reckoned that the one with the trident would reach him about two minutes before the one with the morning star. Holding his sword in readiness he wondered if he would be able to kill the first one in two minutes.

The first Egyptian stepped over the line and advanced slowly. Carroll could not allow this. The fight had to be quickly finished. He leapt forwards flailing his sword from side to side, then staggered back as the prong of the trident grazed his ribs. He saw an opportunity then and stepped forwards once again to invite attack. The Egyptian stabbed at him once again. He moved slightly to one side, the prong of the trident again grazing his ribcage, then he closed his arm down on the trident and caught its haft in his armpit. The Egyptian tugged at it and too late realized this was the wrong thing to do. Carroll's sword came down and gashed his arm through to the bone. The man staggered away trying to stem the flow of blood, his face twisted with shock.

Carroll turned the trident as the second Egyptian entered the area he was set to defend and threw it like a spear. It entered below his opponent's sternum. With a look of surprise the man fell back and sat down, then his expression changed with his awareness of pain to come. Carroll did not give him a chance to suffer that pain. He stepped in close, and putting as much force behind the blow as he could, split the unfortunate man's head in two. He then turned to the one he had wounded. There was a pool of blood gathering below his gashed arm and obvious impatience in his expression.

'Hurry,' intoned Carroll's translator. For a moment Carroll could not understand what he meant. Then, as the man closed his eyes then and tilted his head to one side, Carroll realized that this man wanted a quick death. Carroll quickly obliged him then, after collecting up the spare weapons moved as far from the two corpses as his area allowed. Behind him dull thuds marked the ignition of the two corpses and he turned to see them burning brightly, spewing oily smoke into the air and tainting it with a smell like roasting pork. Carroll swallowed bile.

Time passed slowly as seated at the edge of the four hexagons Carroll waited for instructions, meanwhile watching distant pillars of smoke and distant combats, and listening to the clashing of weapons and to the screams. Julius and the Masai were sent elsewhere and no more opponents came against before the General contacted him.

'Move to the red hexagon within your defensive perimeter.'

Carroll stood and obeyed, keeping to the other side of the hexagon away from the smoking and blackened remains of one of the Egyptians. As soon as he stood upon that hexagon the perimeter line disappeared with a brilliant flash.

'Advance now as indicated by the light on your wristband.'

Carroll studied his wristband then moved to the yellow hexagon adjacent, and so advanced: the trident in his left hand, the sword in his right, and the morning star hanging by its thong from his belt.

And so advanced the nightmare.

The next two opponents matched against him – a turbaned fakir and shaven-headed Nubian – stood little chance against him. With both of them he threw the trident first to mortally wound then moved in to finish the job with the sword. On both occasions he felt sickened and relieved. After dealing with them he was sent chasing a yellow line again then set to defend four hexagons. This time no-one came up against him and after a wait of half an hour or more he was moved on a hexagon at a time. Now the game-board was changing as from hexagon to hexagon he had to step up a couple of inches and, far ahead, surrounded by pillars of smoke like bars, stood a small peak. When this peak became clearer to him through the hazy twilight he felt a vague stirring of recognition, of excitement, of deja vu. A shiver of horripilation ran up his back and for no immediately apparent reason he turned in the direction of his most recent combat. Standing near the blackened and smoking husk of a man was a spectral figure, a figure through which smoke passed undisturbed: the Clown.

Carroll stared at the figure for a moment then said, 'Well?'

The Clown's reply gusted: rose and fell, advanced and retreated like a spring breeze. Carroll only caught a few of the words but the meaning came over clear.

'...voice ... physical ... presence.'

The Clown's voice was as tenuous as his physical presence, this, Carroll realized was the essence of what he was being told.

'You want to tell me something though,' said Carroll.

By the movement of the Clown's lips Carroll could now see that he repeating something over and over again, and he damned himself for not taking the lip-reading course that had once been offered him.

'Win... freedom...' were the only words he heard, and as he heard those words the Clown faded out of existence. Carroll took the words one way only, and he fought.

A samurai died with the trident in his throat. A Zulu warrior died with the broken end of Carroll's sword in his ribs and provided Carroll with a knife which he threw at his next opponent, a Nubian, whose skull Carroll shattered with the morning star. At the foot of the peak he slew a Red Indian, but not before that one put a cut across his chest, and bleeding, he gazed up at what he presumed to be his destination.

The peak curved up like the roof of a pagoda or a Chinese hat. It rose in steps, each step being a hexagon, and these steps getting progressively higher. Here the concentrated fighting filled the air with thick smoke and the reek of burning flesh. And shortly Carroll contributed to it. Three smoking corpses marked the path he had been directed along up the slope. He was luckier than them, not just because he had won, but because he had something to fight for other than to prevent pain.

As Carroll jumped up the two foot step to the next occupied hexagon he hurled his trident at the half-seen figure thereon. There was a clang and the trident went spinning away through the smoke. Once on the hexagon Carroll advanced with a sword and dagger he had recently acquired. The Egyptian who faced him with a small mace and scimitar seemed familiar.

'You,' said Carroll.

'You,' Ramses mimicked, his smile haughty.

Carroll moved in, wary of thrown weapons.

'It is a trick I use infrequently,' said Ramses, on discerning the reason for Carroll's wariness. 'A trick that can only be used against someone who's guard is down.'

Carroll replied with a sweeping cut at Ramses' head, followed by an attempt to plant the dagger in his gut. With a clang and a blur of steel the sword-blow was deflected, and Ramses casually dodged the knife. He then attacked with mace and scimitar in rapid succession. Steel rang and clattered and sparks flew from honed edges. He did not break through Carroll's guard though. In a moment they parted and circled.

'You see, it would have been stupid of me to have thrown away one of my weapons. I would surely have been dead by now.' The Egyptian was panting only slightly.

'Do you want to escape from all this?' Carroll countered. Ramses launched a sudden vicious attack which nearly broke through Carroll's guard. He only pulled back when Carroll managed to slice his arm..

'I am a god!' he yelled angrily, then punctuating his words with swipes of his mace and scimitar, 'Where are my riches? Where... are... my... slaves?'

On the last word Carroll saw an opening and stabbed with his sword. The opening closed and he retreated with a cut on in arm in exactly the same place as the one he had given.

'Cut for cut,' said Ramses.

Carroll decided to try something.

'The Clown knows,' he said, 'he knows of riches and slaves and men who claim to be gods.' His words had more effect than his blows had been having.

Instead of carrying through an attack he had initiated Ramses pulled back with an expression of confused half-comprehension on his face. It had been a mistake to pull back at that point, one that Carroll took advantage of. His sword went in and out of the Pharoah's throat in an incarnadine splash. Ramses staggered back gurgling. As he sank to the ground he stared at Carroll accusingly.

'I'm sorry,' said Carroll, 'but he said I should win,' then he checked his wristband and moved on.

Nearing the top of the peak Carroll saw it was surmounted by one large hexagon. As he drew closer he spotted charred remains all around it, and even as he watched, a man rolled over the side sheathed in blood and flickers of nascent flame.

'You have one opponent yet to face. Beat him and for the first time in seven hundred games Anubis will have been defeated. This could mean much for you, Jason Carroll,' so said the General.

Seven hundred games, thought Carroll, *so nice of him to let me know.* It was a moment before he noticed the Clown standing nearby, and this time the words came clear.

'This close, is enough,' said the Clown, then began to fade away.

'Wait!' shouted Carroll, but the Clown was gone. Filled with trepidation Carroll hauled himself up onto the final hexagon.

The white top hexagon was three times the area of the ones below. At its centre, in a curious contorted framework of silver rods, was suspended a disc of translucent red material about four feet across with a hole through its centre. It appeared to be an expanded version of the discs the Reaper had possession of. It also looked like a gong. Carroll wracked his brains. When had he heard a gong being mentioned? He could not remember, and he did not have the time to try and remember, because his last opponent was coming for him.

He was an old man: short, balding, and wiry, with skin like that of a pickled walnut. White cataracts covered his eyes, and his head was turned slightly to one side as he listened to locate Carroll's position. He wore only a loincloth, and his only weapons were his spade-like hands and feet. Carroll felt his confidence undermined at once. He had seen all the films. This man could only be the master of some obscure martial art.

The old man shambled forwards, his legs bowed and his hands at his sides. Carroll moved to his left, taking his dagger in his right hand. The man was blind. How could he defend himself against a thrown blade? Carroll flipped the dagger over, caught it by its point, and threw. For a moment he thought it would find its target, but then the old man's hand blurred through the air and with a thwack the dagger skittered off the side of the hexagon. Carroll continued to move round the edge.

The old man, he noticed, was keeping between him and the gong. He did not attack; he merely maintained his position. Carroll decided that it was up to him to initiate violence, though he was reluctant to. He closed in, swinging his sword. The old man's hands blurred again and again turning away every cut

41

Carroll tried to deliver. He did not see the blow that struck him in the chest. Suddenly found himself falling to the ground with a deep aching pain across his sternum and his breath whooshing out. As he hit the ground he realized he had lost his sword. He managed to push himself upright to search for it, in time to see it slashing through the air towards him. The thing he always remembered afterwards was that it hurt more when his head hit the ground than when it got separated from his body. Death came swiftly, but he still had time to see blood frothing from the neck of his own convulsing corpse.

Chapter Four

'He cheats,' said a voice out of the blackness.

'Who?' asked Carroll dreamily.

'Anubis. You do not think that was a man you faced in the last hexagon do you?'

'What was he then?'

'It,' corrected the voice Carroll now recognized as the Clown's, 'it is a machine.'

'A robot?'

'The term android is preferable I think, as in a machine shaped like a human.'

Carroll made no reply as he became aware of redness slowly resolving into a strange landscape. He found himself sitting on a rock.

'Who are you?' he eventually asked.

'I will tell you a story,' said the Clown. His voice issued from all around. Carroll could not locate its source.

He interrupted. 'Where are you?'

'I am all around you. The information that is you has been entrapped by the information that is me, and mine exists in my soul disc.'

'The gong,' Carroll stated, and gazed out at the flat red land below the flat red sky. 'This is not my body then... or rather, at this moment I do not have a body?'

'The latter is correct. I thought you would be more comfortable holding your present form and thus created this representation for you.'

'You are right' this is more comfortable for me. Tell me your story, then.'

'Once upon a time–'

'Cut the crap.'

'Very well,' said the Clown with wry humour, then after a long pause continued, 'Before your planet had even condensed out of the cloud of debris and gas that formed your solar system, when your sun was newly ignited and on its first circuit of the galaxy, there was an ageless being born of an mortal race, a sport, a mutation. This one lived for so long that, perhaps by chance, it was inevitable he would become a master of the arts of survival, and so he did. For him agelessness became practical immortality, nothing short of being caught in a supernova could destroy him, and so he lived, lived for eons – long enough to see the race that bore him slide into extinction.'

In his pretend body on the pretend rock Carroll found himself without any emotional response to the Clown's words. Here was a story too far from all he knew and understood. The Clown went on, his words falling into the pretend air like stones.

'After this happened the immortal being cursed himself for not finding some way to have conferred immortality onto his fellows. He lived in loneliness for a time, and had he been less of a survivor he might have gone mad, but even that escape was denied him. He then he built himself a space ship and went in search of other intelligent life. He searched for time impossible for you to comprehend and all he found were the beginnings of life – worlds where the heights of evolutionary achievement were planktons and slimes. Eventually he ceased searching, and over those worlds he had found he set watchers, machines that sought, probed, and tested for sentient life, machines that sometimes accelerated the mechanism of evolution, and as they did this he set about building a titanic construct, for he now knew that the life born on those worlds would be mortal like his forebears...'

44

'The construct he built was a disc around a sun; a home for untold billions. It was his intention to record the beings that would one day ascend from the life he had seen and place them in new ageless bodies on the disc, so that they would have time to develop, to evolve mentally into suitable companions for himself. And so he waited, unaware that he had already created sentient beings and that they plotted against him.'

'Out of necessity he had built robots to help him; mechanical intelligences. As the millennia passed, they evolved into something more than he had made them. Through accident chance, copying errors in their programs they came to think of themselves as gods and they came to covet power. And so, as the first intelligences came to be on your planet, and as the first recordings were made, they set about making a recording of their builder and, before he could resurrect any of the intelligences recorded, they destroyed his ship, his body, and entrapped his life-field in the recording of himself so that he could not remake his body.'

A long silence ensued while Carroll digested that. *What am I?* He wondered. *Am I a copy of a copy of a copy? What is Jason Carroll? Is he mind or is he soul? Does such a thing as the soul exist?*

'Recording,' he repeated uneasily, 'what am I? Do I have a soul? You said something about a soul disc...'

'Does it matter? From year to year a living being is not the same being. The material of its body has been exchanged for different material. Its mind has decayed and found new ways of working. You are information continually undergoing change. That information is recorded. If you had a soul then it resides now in some heaven for I have never found such. Here the essence of you is a small disc made from one long information carrying molecule. I call them soul discs out of arbitrary choice. I see no better use for the word.'

Carroll could think of no reply. He did not believe in gods yet he found it difficult to visualize himself merely as information, yet, what was his DNA?

'Robots,' he said, getting back to the story, 'I presume these are games players?'

The Clown answered him in a voice with something in it that made his spine crawl.   'Yes, and now they play games with a few of the intelligences recorded. This must not continue.'

It was obvious to Carroll who the builder of the disc was so he asked the one question he now thought was expected of him. 'How then do we discontinue it?'

'I can do nothing but advise you between those times when my soul disc is rung, for now anyway. It is you, Jason Carroll, who must act.'

'What can I do?'

'You can destroy the present form of the Reaper and completely destroy the General. Once this is done you will have time to escape. You must take your soul disc and flee towards the sun.'

'My soul disc,' said Carroll, realizing now, 'in that box on the arm of the Reaper's throne.' He laughed. 'And all I have to do is destroy the Reaper and the General. I hate to disappoint you but that is not all that simple –'

The Clown interrupted, 'A gun is not a gun when it is a billet of metal and therefore is not a weapon. It is potentially a weapon though. Sulphur, potassium nitrate and charcoal are not gun powder when separate.'

'Kruger asked for a gun, Ellery for a hand-grenade,' said Carroll, catching the Clown's meaning immediately. 'Is this why you've chosen me? My training, my knowledge?'

'Yes, you are a resourceful man Jason Carroll, and you can find weapons where no other can. It is not often that one such as yourself is chosen for the game, as normally the four select those from eras where edged weapons were predominant. The Reaper chose so many from the twentieth century this time in an attempt to find a way to win, but of course with Anubis's android on the final hexagon the Reaper will not succeed.'

Carroll nodded. 'So I junk the Reaper and the General and flee for the sunset. That's it?'

'No, remember your soul disc, and be advised that they are indestructible and to each person his own seems blue.'

'I'll do as you say then. What other choices do I have?' said Carroll, standing up, 'Now, how the Hell do I get out of here?'

'Simple,' said the Clown, and blackness descended like a falling wall.

Chapter Five

As before, there was a metallic taste in his mouth, and as before, a line of light appeared to one side of him. The door to the resurrection booth swung open and he stumbled out into unchanged twilight. Julius was waiting for him this time, and from the building came the sounds of shouting, drunken singing, and the occasional snatch of music, mournful music.

'You are the last through,' said the legionary, handing Carroll a skirt-like garment like the one he wore. Carroll donned it in a daze, befuddled by his conversation with the Clown and wondering just how he was going to deal with the Reaper and the General. He gazed across to where they stood facing each other – the Reaper on his throne and the General with his swagger stick tucked under his arm. It occurred to him then that knowing they were machines did not make facing dealing with them any easier. He knew just how effective a machine could be. His encounter with Anubis's android had shown him that. Then he laughed. Of course. Against the android he had only limited time and hand weapons. Now he could do better than that. With the perplexed legionary trailing behind he headed for the building. There was something he had to try.

Within the building the scene was the same as after the last game. Everyone was getting drunk and stoned and the air was redolent with the smokes from various narcotics. Carroll acknowledged Ellery, who shouted at him drunkenly then continued to deal the cards he held while puffing out clouds of cigar smoke. The card players, Carroll noted, were gambling with gold and silver coins, worthless here. He did not join them, and instead he went to his creation booth and typed in

'Potassium Nitrate, 1lb'. The light on the side of the cylinder came on then went off and Carroll removed a sealed paper bag which he opened, dipped his finger in, and tasted. He then grinned and typed in for a couple of carrier bags then all sorts of other things that could be purchased from a chemist's shop. He then went on to get himself some more combat clothing as the garment Julius had given him was not his idea of dressed. When he had all he wanted, he glanced round at the legionary.

'Come on, I'll need your help,' he said, then looked up and signalled to Ellery. The American nodded, and Carroll and Julius headed for one of the rooms.

Once the three of them were together in a room, Ellery slumped drunkenly on one of the fold down beds, and Julius leaning against the wall with a cigarette in his mouth, Carroll emptied the contents of the bags on the floor, then put on the clothes he had brought. Ellery lifted himself up onto his elbows and stared at the packets blearily.

'Mothballs, sugar, bleach, what? You're re-stocking the bathroom?'

'No,' said Carroll, 'I'm getting out of here.'

'Oh yeah?'

'Yes.' Carroll looked round at Julius. 'You remember I told you about bombs, well with these ingredients I can make bombs.'

'Oh shit!' said Ellery and slumped back on the bed again.

Carroll went on, 'And with these bombs I intend to convert the Reaper and the General to scrap.'

'Scrap?' repeated Julius, his eyes on the packages on the floor.

'Yes, you see, they are robots... A Clown told me so...'

And then Carroll told them of his dreams, his fight to the centre of the game-board and his last encounter with the enigmatic Clown. As he spoke he finished dressing then seated himself on the floor to mix and crush together powders, pour and stir in liquids, to strain and heat and blend in the manner he had been taught. His proficiency was of a soldier trained to manufacture weapons of sabotage on enemy territory. As he worked he also told them of the soul discs, what they were and how they appeared to the individual. At length he finished his story, and at length he finished his work and had three blocks of a soap-like substance which he carefully wrapped in oiled paper. By that time the sounds of drunken revelry had finished and Ellery had reached a state of tired sobriety. Carroll then went on to
make fuses while Ellery and Julius asked the inevitable questions. Ellery was sceptical.

'How d'you know this Clown ain't like the Reaper, that he ain't playing games with you as well?'

'I don't,' replied Carroll, 'but how would I get proof that this is not the case, and what other options are there? If we do nothing we will continue to be pieces in a board-game, dying painfully each time it is played, forever, or until the Reaper decides to trade us in for different pieces. I for one am prepared to try and get free of that, prepared to gamble a few minutes of agony against freedom and practical immortality.'

'If the punishment for such an attempt is only a few minutes of agony, and if this Clown is telling the truth,' said Julius.

'I am prepared to believe. I do not want to believe that there is no escape. Our situation here is intolerable,' said Carroll, then glanced up to see that Julius was edging towards the door. Julius held his hands up to his ears and flapped them then pointed at the door.

'You want us to help you then,' said Ellery, seeing what was happening and adding his bit to keep the conversation going.

'That was the idea, but it's up to you,' said Carroll as he stood up and moved to the door also, 'either way the General and the Reaper get blown up and I'm grabbing my disc and running.' As he spoke his last word Julius yanked the door open.

Kruger was caught completely by surprise, and as the door came open he stumbled into the room.

'I will not tell' I will not tell! Let me come with you!' he shouted as Julius caught him in a headlock and seemed prepared to break his neck.

'Kill him,' said Ellery as he stepped off of the bunk.

'No,' said Carroll, picking up the three bombs.

'Why not?' snarled Ellery, 'we can't trust him, he'll go straight to the Reaper.'

'I know,' said Carroll reasonably, 'but what happens to him if we kill him?'

'Resurrected,' said Julius relaxing his grip on the SS officer's neck.

Kruger coughed and repeated, 'Let me come with you.'

Carroll stared at him and he lapsed into silence. Carroll turned to Ellery. 'Tie him up. You're with me now I think?'

Julius and Ellery nodded in agreement.

'I'll go get some rope,' said Ellery and he exited the room.

'Honestly, I will not tell, I only told before because I could see no other way to freedom.'

Carroll squatted down in front of him and studied him carefully. 'I do not think you would be prepared to risk punishment, Kruger. Perhaps I am wrong, but I think that you feel you have more to gain by taking sides with the Reaper and the General. I am afraid that I cannot afford to take the risk of trusting you.' With that he nodded to Julius who forced Kruger face-down onto the floor. Kruger did not struggle, knowing now that nothing worse than being tied up was going to happen to him.

When Ellery returned with rope Carroll cut and attached fuses to the bombs, leaving the other two to deal with Kruger.

'He won't be going anywhere,' said Ellery when he and Julius finally dumped Kruger on the bed.

'Here,' said Carroll, passing them a bomb each. He then took out a packet of cigarettes and offered them. 'After touching a lighted cigarette to the fuse you have approximately three seconds.' He demonstrated with an unlit cigarette for Julius's benefit, then he said to Ellery alone, 'Just like a grenade.'

Ellery grunted without humour as they left the room.

It seemed to take forever for them to reach the doors of the building, but when they finally stepped out they came upon a scene that put their hasty plans into disarray. A throne was ascending from the sky, a throne much the same as the Reaper's but containing a being of wholly different appearance. The one seated there had the body of a huge powerful man and the head of a jackal. Anubis had come for a visit.

'Shit!' hissed Carroll and remembered the last time his only comment on events had been thus, just before a bus wheel had crushed his chest. He and his companions halted and watched as the throne howled in to landing, nearly crushing the General who was forced to leap out of the way.

'Okay, we're spectators. Act like a spectator,' said Carroll.

Ellery lounged back against the wall with his hand, containing a bomb, tucked into the capacious pocket of his fatigues. Carroll leant back against the wall as well, his bomb tucked into the front of his shirt. All his plans were now coming apart. Should he try to get Anubis as well? Should he wait until Anubis went away, and if so, how long should he wait? How far away would Anubis go? How quickly could he return? Carroll gazed out across the steel plain. There was nowhere to hide out there and if one of the four came after him they would find him with ease.

'Let's go back inside,' he said, and the three of them returned inside the building and seated themselves at a table near the door. With sweat sticking his clothing to him Carroll stared out into the twilight.

Between the Reaper and Anubis there seemed to be no verbal exchange and Carroll was at a loss to know what they were doing. Being machines they could surely communicate things to each other in seconds? It was difficult though to draw comparisons between these two the robots and computers he knew. As he watched them, seated there facing each other, the sheer weirdness of the scene became almost overpowering. Here was the jackal-headed death-god of the Egyptians facing a medieval personification of death. Both of them were seated on thrones that moved as if powered by turbines. Both of them had the power they were reputed to have in myth. And both of them were machines older than human history.

Carroll wondered then if the forms they possessed now were the same forms they had possessed all those eons in the past. He wondered if the myths had somehow arisen from them, or they had altered themselves to the shape of myth.

Abruptly, as he took two cards from the cigarette puffing Julius, Carroll's tension cycled to a new level. In the distance, beyond the Reaper and Anubis, two black dots had appeared in the sky, rapidly growing closer.

'Looks like my timing is about as much use as an ashtray on a motorbike,' he said succinctly.

Ellery let out a noise that might have been a bark of laughter or an exclamation of pain and Julius examined them both queryingly. Carroll nodded towards the doors. Outside, another throne, along with a floating dais, were dropping from the sky.

'What d'you reckon?' asked Ellery.

Carroll shrugged. 'We could go out there and watch, but I don't think we'll learn very much.'

Ellery nodded and threw his cards in. The three of them stood up and went outside. With them came the Masai and the Cavalier. Then shortly after that came the rest.

The Four faced each other in silence: Kali, the Hindu goddess of destruction, a woman with greenish skin, six arms, strangely sinuous and erotic yet with eyes that seemed to be enamel; Quetzalcoatl, a huge serpent coiled on its dais, a foot thick and fifteen long with multi-coloured feathers instead of scales, a crest of feathers, huge snake eyes, and a crocodilian mouth full of hooked teeth; Anubis, the man with a black jackal head; And the skeletal Reaper.

No speech was audible from them yet it seemed to Carroll that there must be some harsh debate in progress. It lasted for a good ten minutes and Carroll wondered what sort of language these machines might use that required so long to exchange information. Yet, if what the Clown had told him was true it might well be that this exchange was so long because of the lies being told.

At the end of the ten minutes the Reaper held up one bony hand and clacked its fingers together. Annubis's jackal

54

head snapped back and its mouth opened. Between white teeth a very realistic tongue lolled. It slammed its huge hands down on the scrolled arms of its throne, which lifted from the ground with an abrupt roar, its back-blast knocking the General from his feet.

'What the hell was that about?' wondered Ellery, 'Looks like he went off in a huff.'

'Perhaps they caught him cheating,' said Carroll and peered up to where Anubis had brought his throne to a wavering halt. The throne rotated until it was facing out over the game-board, a stuttering flash of red arc-light became visible, then the throne began to settle.

'Somebody just burnt,' said Ellery.

'Yes,' said Carroll, 'and I would bet we will see who in a moment.'

As Anubis's throne clumped to the ground the jackal-headed god gestured at the resurrection machine. The door of the machine thumped open and a wizened figure stepped out. The old man was oriental in appearance and had blind white eyes.

'That the one..?' asked Ellery.

Carroll nodded as he backed away and tried to make himself appear less visible. He had a bad feeling about this. He reached into his pocket and touched the lump of explosive as if for reassurance. The waxed paper was slimy. Carroll swallowed dryly.

Things were not good, they were not good at all.

'Be careful,' he whispered to Ellery, 'damn bombs are sweating nitro—' He stopped talking when he saw the Reaper's head swivelling in their direction. Abruptly the General, off to one side, jerked as if someone had tugged his strings, then tucked his swagger stick under one arm and marched over to stand before the men. Carroll returned his attention to the Reaper and started to remove the explosive from his pocket. It would have to be now. They stood no chance, but if the Reaper knew...

'Jason Carroll,' said the General lifting his swagger stick, 'step forwards.'

Carroll found he could do nothing but obey. The bomb dropped back into his pocket. By this time the old oriental had reached Anubis's throne Carroll realized there was something different about him. He seemed slower, more careful, more like someone who was blind. The General lowered his swagger stick as Carroll came to stand before him.

'You will fight this man of Anubis's. Should you beat him your rewards could be great.'

'I already fought him once. He beat me,' said Carroll. He did not need this now. He did not need this at all.

The General was silent for a moment, glassy eyed, seemingly staring through him. Then he said, 'The one you fought was not this one.'

Carroll nodded, so, Anubis had been caught cheating. 'What weapons do we use?' Again the General was silent for a time before replying, as if everything he said was coming directly from the Reaper.

'There will be no weapons, as there is some doubt as to the weapons present when you fought originally.'

Great, though Carroll, one up for Anubis there.

'May I have a moment to prepare?' asked Carroll.

'You may,' replied the General after a glassy-eyed silence.

Carroll turned and headed back to Ellery and Julius. 'Here,' he handed his explosive to Ellery, 'our plans have been put back, but not altered.' He sat down and began to take off his boots.

'Do you think you can win against this man?' asked Julius.

'I have a chance, now that he is only a man,' said Carroll, and once his boots were off he went immediately into some vigorous stretching exercises. He did not know how long he had. As he dropped down into box splits he gazed across at his opponent. The old oriental was squatting like a casual gargoyle. Carroll did not like the look of him at all.

'Luck to you, Jason Carroll.'

Carroll glanced around and saw the Masai and the Cavalier standing behind him.

'I will need it I think,' he said, and stood up. When he scanned around he noted that all the fighters were glancing between him and the oriental. He wondered if any bets were being made, and if so what the odds were. With his feet bare he got into a fighting stance and bounced back and forth. The surface was good, better than some of the dojos he had trained in. He hoped he would do his instructors proud. He stepped out towards his opponent.

'Are you now ready to begin?' asked the General.

'Ready enough,' said Carroll, and as he said it the oriental's head snapped round in his direction and he rose to his feet.

The General said, 'There are no rules, no time limit. This is a fight to the death. You may begin.'

Carroll and the oriental approached each other and circled, the oriental with his head tilted to one side as if listening, yet, observing him, Carroll reckoned he was not wholly blind. It occurred to him that he must not assume blindness at all, Anubis being a known cheat. He closed, carefully.

Throwing two body punches and two head punches in rapid succession showed Carroll that the oriental was fast but not infallible. He dodged the first three with unnatural speed, but the last connected. Yet even that was only a glancing blow to the cheekbone, and Carroll had to step back as hooked fingers stabbed at his eyes then a foot like a gnarled club tried to take his head off. No rules. He had to remember that.

Blind...

Carroll moved close and brought his hands together for a ringing clap. For a moment the oriental seemed confused and in that moment Carroll brought the edge of his foot down on the kneecap of his opponent's leading leg. Something cracked and the oriental seemed to fall backwards. Carroll tried to follow through, but the man's other leg came up blindingly fast and the foot slammed into Carroll's chest like an iron bar. With his breath leaving him, Carroll stumbled back. The oriental did not follow through though. His damaged leg gave way and he stumbled, giving Carroll a moment to recover before they closed again.

They exchanged blows at a speed that made it evident why karate matches require three referees. None connected tellingly until the oriental stumbled on his bad leg and Carroll caught him on the side of his head with the edge of his hand. Then it was over in seconds. Carroll's next twisting karate punch took the oriental in the windpipe. He dropped to his knees choking. Carroll's next punch came down on the base of his skull like a hammer and the man fell bonelessly on his face. Gasping Carroll stepped back.

A silence ensued, shortly broken by Ellery's cheer, then Julius's, then the cheers of the others.

'He is not dead,' said the General, and the cheering slowly died away. Carroll glared with distaste at the General before returning his attention to his felled opponent. He stepped up close, squatted down, took hold of the oriental's head and in one violent movement snapped his neck.

'Satisfied now?' he asked the General as he stood up.

'He is dead now,' said the General.

Carroll looked round at the Four, whereupon Anubis's throne roared and shot into the air. As the jackal-headed god receded out of sight the oriental burst into greasy flame. Carroll turned away and headed back towards Ellery and Julius, reaching them as Kali's throne then Quetzalcoatl's dais followed Anubis's into the twilight.

Once he was back with Julius and Ellery Carroll said, 'He would not have dodged the knife, but that is not important.'

Carefully he sat down and put on his socks and boots. 'What is important is how and when we act.' At that point the Masai, the Cavalier, and the British Redcoat approached.

'We have come to congratulate you for a fine –' began the Redcoat.

'Yes, great, wonderful,' said Carroll, and turned away to enter the building. Julius and Ellery quickly followed. Soon they were seated at one of the tables again while Carroll wrapped an elasticated bandage round his ribs.

'When do we do it?' asked Ellery.

Carroll held out his hand and after a moment Ellery handed him his bomb.

'Deal the cards, Julius,' he said as he pocketed the sweating explosive.

Julius did as bid and they all took up their cards.

'We cannot do it yet. We don't know how quickly the other three can get back here. It would be best to wait until the start of the next game. That way we'll know they are back at their home bases.'

Three hours later the General's summons came.

'Now,' said Carroll, and offered round his cigarettes, 'we go out with the rest and try to get as close to the Reaper and the General as possible, remember, on my signal we go for it. As agreed, you, Ellery, go for the General and you, Julius, go for the Reaper. I'll keep mine back to finish either of them you might miss or not completely scrap. Remember, your discs appear blue to you, don't run without them.'

They stood and joined the fighters leaving the building. Pulling the bombs from concealment they edged towards the General and the Reaper rather than the hexagons indicated by their wristbands. Glancing at his wristband Carroll was surprised to see that neither colour nor number was showing. This then was his reward. From this game he was exempt. But the next? There would be no next.

Suddenly there came a shout from behind. Carroll swore and broke into a run. He did not have to look back to know who had shouted, obviously the extra time had been enough for Kruger to free himself.

Ellery took the lead as they sprinted towards the General and the Reaper. He slid to a halt as the General raised his baton, pulled out his bomb and touched his cigarette to the fuse. As he was doing this Carroll saw the Reaper's skeletal hand shoot into the box on the arm of its throne. Ellery's arm came back for a grenade throw. A stab of ruby light from the Reaper and Ellery became sheathed in flame. He did not have time to scream. His arm continued through its motion and the bomb travelled in a text book arc, then what remained of him slumped to the ground, dead so much quicker than Kruger, as he had burnt in a hotter flame.

Carroll counted as the bomb flew through the air. 'One hundred and one, one hundred and two, on –' He never reached three because the bomb exploded early, a yard from the General's head, which disappeared, and trailing smoke he fell back and hit the ground like a bag of tools. Subliminally Carroll saw exposed and twisted metal, wires and shattered circuitry, and cogs rolling across the ground.

The turbine of the Reaper's throne burst into life just as Julius threw his bomb and Carroll touched his cigarette to the fuse of his. A smoky orange flash knocked the Reaper's throne sideways and blasted his robes away to expose metallic skeleton. It was not enough. Carroll hurled his bomb just as the Reaper fixed its attention on a second disc.

Another stab of ruby light dropped Julius screaming in flames, just before Carroll's bomb blew the Reaper from his throne in smoking pieces. A wreckage of electronics and mechanisms strewed all around, some still falling even as Carroll stepped in amongst them in search of a blue disc. The throne, still partially intact, still had that box on its arm containing most of the discs. Carroll stepped up, searched it, grabbed his own and then turned to the fighters who stood watching in stunned amazement.

'Your own discs are blue! Grab them and run!' he shouted, and then he ran towards the forever setting sun. He did not look back.

Chapter Six

He had run for at least ten miles.

He was sure of this because he felt as exhausted as he used to feel on a training run and that had always been with a twenty pound pack on and over rough terrain, not this unchanging flatness. But then, on those training runs he had not recently fought for his life, though it had not been unusual to run with injuries like the bruised ribs he now had. He glanced back and saw that the building was almost indiscernible now. He looked forwards and wondered just how far he had to go and what his destination was to be. And he ran on, trying not to think of his thirst, and how foolish he had been not to bring supplies.

It was after what had to be least twenty miles when he looked aside and saw the Clown keeping pace with to him. He slowed to a walk.

'I can communicate with you now,' said the Clown. 'The longer they forego that ridiculous disc-ringing ceremony the easier it is for me to do so.'

'Where am I heading?' asked Carroll between gasps.

'To the edge of what you call the steel plain, then beyond. You are close now. Look.' The Clown pointed.

Carroll peered ahead and saw that below the sunset a line could be discerned, a horizon.

'You see, the steel plain is just one face of one of the matter converters I used to construct the solar disc.'

Carroll felt his heart and stomach tighten and he suddenly felt very small. So massive a construction and it was only a tool.

'Matter converter,' he repeated, 'a tool, a machine bigger than a city... How long–' he stopped when he saw the Clown's pained expression and what could only be described as a crack dividing him in two.

'They play the game yet,' said the Clown, and another crack appeared. 'They think you will die just like the rest, that I have no plan–' another crack appeared then another and another, and before Carroll the Clown broke apart, flew to pieces, and disappeared.

What the Hell! thought Carroll, and looked ahead towards the edge of the steel plain. There, very faintly, he could see indistinct shapes. He set out towards them at a trot.

The first shape Carroll came to was a desiccated corpse so far gone with age that when he touched it with is foot it collapsed to dust.

'They think you will die just like the rest.'

He did not know exactly how long it would take for a corpse to get into such a condition in a place like this, but what he did know was that this corpse had been here for a very long time. He moved on, slowing to a walk as he saw another corpse, then another. In all he saw six, two of them burnt, the other four all desiccated. He wondered again about the duration of the game, and he also wondered about the duration of the Clown's game, whatever it might be. How many had died permanently in the Clown's cause? He did not want to be one of their number. He did not want to die again.

Eventually he reached the edge and the last of the shapes. Here stood a resurrection machine, though one very different from those he had seen before. It was comprised of a cylinder approximately seven feet in height and four in diameter, its top a hemisphere and its bottom resting in a vase-like pedestal. Tubes and hexagonal ducts fed into it from all around from sockets in the steel ground. It was predominantly black and silver and its surface was deeply pitted. The door inset into the cylinder confirmed that at it was indeed a resurrection machine, though perhaps a very old one. He approached with a degree of suspicion.

On a yard-high stalk of blackish metal a short distance from the machine stood what looked like a metal sunflower, and which Carroll assumed to be a control console, though he could discern no buttons or switches. A chaotic coloured pattern as from immiscible coloured liquids swirled together decorated its top surface. He reached out to touch this and light ignited under his fingertips and followed their course. Not knowing how this might benefit him or not he stepped past the console to the main machine, only there to find a skeleton slumped at its base.

'What were you promised then?' he asked in a cracked voice.

The skeleton leant up against a cluster of tubes that disappeared like the roots of a tree into the ground. It was curled up with his knees up against his chest and his ragged clothes pulled tightly around it as if against cold. Empty eye sockets gazed up at Carroll. *Why?* Carroll turned away with a shudder, his throat dry with thirst and his body weak with exhaustion. Why had this one decayed and the others merely dried out?

He walked away from it to the edge and a breeze of moisture laden air gave him his answer like a taunt. An increase in the dampness of the air had allowed the corpse to go through the slow process of decay by the bacteria it carried, unlike those corpses further back. It seemed a horrible irony to Carroll, considering that this man had probably died of thirst. He shook his head and looked down.

The steel surface dropped at ninety degrees to the horizontal. The steel plain ended in a steel cliff. Carroll squatted down and touched the edge, the corner. It was sharp, almost as if freshly machined. From that edge the cliff dropped down into mistiness. Far below the ground was grey, mottled with large patches of red. *More steel?* Though Carroll wondered if it was truly steel he stood upon. He was beginning to doubt it could be anything so prosaic.

The mottled grey and red extended to a sunrise only slightly higher than before. There was nothing else. Of course, Carroll realized, if the Clown was telling the truth, and he saw no reason to doubt that he was, then ninety odd million miles of plain lay between here and the very edge of the sun. He moved away from the edge with a hollow feeling in the pit of his stomach and unquestioning awe. What now? Where was the Clown? He moved back to the resurrection machine and sat down with his back against a cluster of tubes. His position in repose was exactly the same as the skeleton's.

Red were the bars that caged him, red the prison, red the sky above and red the ground below. All colour and substance extended in discs around him. He was trapped, held as he had been held so many times before. But this time he had to be free. This time there were things he had to do. He reached through the gauzy fabrics of space, round all that enclosed him, to tap energy he had spent many years accumulating and had been waiting for many years to employ. The bars crumpled. The rings broke and fell away. And he was free, hurtling above a patchwork of hexagons where men died and burnt, then hurtling above an expanse of a substance like steel, but which was infinitely stronger.

♠♠♠

'About time,' said Carroll, getting unsteadily to his feet. His voice was hoarse, his face sick white, and his eyes red rimmed. He had been waiting for too long. He knew he was dying of thirst.

The image of the Clown hovered before him seemingly stronger than it had ever been before, its bell-toed shoes hovering a foot off of the ground. 'You have your disc?' he asked, and this time his voice possessed power.

Carroll nodded and took out and displayed his disc. The Clown slid to one side and came to a bobbing halt beside the console. 'Quickly, here!'

Carroll staggered over to stand next to the Clown.

'Place your disc here,' the Clown directed his attention to a small slot in the top of the console. Carroll did as bid. The disc sank halfway into the slot. 'Touch your fingers now to red, green, red, blue, yellow, then red and blue together.'

Carroll reached down and woodenly stabbed his fingers at the coloured patches. As he hit the last to colours the disc dropped into the console and he felt a wrenching sensation in the pit of his stomach. He fell against the console, gasping.

'Quickly now, enter the machine,' said the Clown, and as he said this he peered up and to the side. Carroll followed the direction of his gaze and saw something silhouetted against the starlit sky, something lit by the occasional flickers of ruby light. He pushed himself from the console and moved drunkenly to the machine. The door stood half open. He entered, taking one last look at the object in the sky. It was a throne he realized as the door closed upon him; a throne in which was seated a manlike form with the head of a jackal.

Suddenly a crashing explosion shook the machine, instantly overlaid by a flash of white and heat and a sense of dislocation, sickening in its intensity. Then the door opened and he was somewhere else.

Carroll reeled forwards and out, the skin of his face loosening with the touch of airborne moisture and his ears popping because of a sudden change of pressure. He glanced up expecting to see Anubis bearing down on him and instead saw a steel cliff reaching up into starlit space and curving away on either side to be lost into misty distant. He took a pace forwards and something crunched under his boots like shingle. Then he realized: *boots.*

Somehow he had been transported, clothing as well. He gazed back at the booth in wonderment and there saw a flash of blue on its floor, unsteadily he reached back inside and grabbed up his soul disc and placed it in his pocket. It would not do to lose his life. Next something else penetrated the haze of his mind and he peered down again. Shingle? No, not shingle, but soul discs, millions of soul discs. Carroll felt numb and just stood staring at the ground in vacuous confusion.

'Towards the sun,' came the Clown's voice out of the air after a time that could have been minutes or hours to Carroll. He checked around him and could see no sign of his eldritch guide. What he did see though, and what impinged on his awareness more than all else, was a pool of scummy water gathered in a depression in the grey ground. He went to the pool and drank his fill.

Almost immediately his head cleared, and once sated he sat on a pile of soul discs and gazed across their scattered redness into the distance. From the cliff those red areas had appeared vast. *One disc for every human to have died on Earth?* He drank more of the metallic tasting water then stood and walked on. He was not surprised when on his way he passed two more corpses, bones gleaming whitely and flesh fallen away like something washed up on a beach. These, Carroll realized, were more recent. Such was the way of it. He wondered if he would be joining their number to pave the way for some other to walk on this sunset path.

♠♠♠

For how long or for how far he walked Carroll had no idea. He drank frequently at the many pools, gradually rehydrating himself, and he walked. Once he stopped to lie down upon a pile of soul discs. Then on waking he walked again. In time the cliff became a small square object behind him almost hidden by the haze that seemed to hang over everything. And the further he got from it the more disconcerted he became. As strange as the game board was it seemed familiar now in retrospect. He could not judge the passage of time because the sun did not move, and he could not judge distance because there was no curve to the horizon. All around him the red and grey ground disappeared into immeasurable distances.

After a time he could not judge he saw something far ahead of him which he at first took to be illusory. Eventually it stayed constantly in his sights and he knew it was real, though it seemed to be moving. When he got closer he heard a gravelly crunching and the whine of electric motors. At first he considered avoiding this thing, then he decided he did not care. Soon it came clearly into view: a machine like a huge insect mounted no shiny serrated wheels. He watched as with slow deliberation it rolled forwards picking up soul discs one at a time in tweezers at the end of its front appendages, placing them in a slot mouth as if to taste them, then spitting them out and moving on to the next. He watched it for a while then moved on. Was it searching for specific discs? He gazed around at the redness stretching into hazy distance and wondered how many it had checked, and how many it had left to do. The he left it to its task and went on his way.

Hunger became his constant bane, but all he could do was fill his gut with water and walk on. Twice more he fell asleep on piles of soul discs, there to have nightmares in which the only thing he remembered was the fear. Eventually there came a time when he sat down on a pile of soul discs and found no inclination to get up again. Almost as if this was what he had been watching for the Clown reappeared.

'And where have you been?' Carroll asked hoarsely.

'Leading Anubis astray,' replied the Clown.

Carroll nodded blankly and stared into the distance. It seemed to draw his eyes from his head. He snapped his gaze away.

'People could never live here,' he said with an edge to his voice, vaguely aware that he had forgotten something important.

The Clown gestured at the surrounding desolation. 'This is not what I intended. The Four trapped me before I had time to finish my creation.'

'Yeah,' said Carroll noncommittally, feeling annoyed and sorry for himself. 'Why are you a Clown? Is it because you like practical jokes? The kind that end up leaving corpses scattered across your creation?'

'Before the Four trapped me in my soul disc my form was very much different from this–'

'Yeah,' Carroll interrupted, then bowed his head to stare at the green scummy water around his feet. 'Saw a machine earlier ... it was searching... I think.'

69

'Yes, it was a library robot that survived the ruin of my ship. All the discs were kept together there in chronological order, and the robot is trying to do the job it did there ... trying to keep the discs in order.'

Carroll glanced up. 'What's it looking for?'

'The disc of the first sentient on your planet.'

'And when it has found that?'

'It will look for the second.'

Carroll shook his head and rested it in his hands. Such awe inspiring futility, he could think of nothing more to ask about it, but that the robot did search like that posed another interesting question.

'How do the Four get their discs ... like ... me?'

'When they destroyed my ship sections of the library came down intact. All that you see around you is a small portion of the whole. But library collections do not apply to you. Your disc, like the discs of some of your fellows, were ones recently recorded and taken directly from the receiver.'

'Receiver–' began Carroll, and wished he had not.

'Yes, a gravity pulse receiver within the solar disc. The main recorder is in what is called the red spot on the planet Jupiter of your solar system. It records each of you then transmits the information here.'

Carroll tried not to think too much about that. 'Where the Hell am I going?' he asked instead.

'You are going to my ship,' replied the Clown.

Carroll took that in and went on, 'And why am I going to your ship? Not to re-catalogue your library I hope.'

'You are going to my ship to get weapons, equipment, whatever you may require to steal my soul disc.'

'I see.' Carroll took his head out of his hands.

Weapons and equipment were words that revived him. He knew what to do with weapons...

'How far away is your ship?' he said, standing up.

'Fifty miles,' replied the Clown, and Carroll groaned.

The Clown went on, 'There will be food and drink there as well. Can you walk fifty miles?'

'Yeah, I guess I'll have to,' he said. Couldn't you have put that transporter thing nearer to your ship?'

'No, because I did not put it there. There are many like it scattered across the whole disc, but they are thousands of miles apart. That one was the nearest.'

Carroll nodded. 'You always have an explanation.' But he was not thinking about what he was saying. The Clown's previous mention of food was making his mouth water. Still nodding he drifted, staring at the non-horizon.

'My ship is there,' said the Clown. Carroll turned to gaze where the Clown was pointing, to the left of the sun. There he was able to discern something, hazily. It did not occur to him until he started walking that if he could see it from fifty miles away then it must be immense.

Chapter Seven

It looked like the beached remains of some titanic cetacean: a great grey mass of improbable immensity with exposed ribs at its highest point, reaching into the sky like claws, but clad with metal plates lower down, clinging to them like mummified skin. Ahead lay a gigantic engine something like an airliner's turbine, and as Carroll drew closer to it, stepping amongst lesser wreckage strewn all about, he wondered what the Four had done to bring this leviathan down.

The torn and shattered of machinery scattered on the ground amidst the soul discs looked like nothing Earthly. Its component parts did not have the square order of human built machines, rather, they were close packed and rounded like organs, and were connected with what looked like veins, arteries, and intestinal tubes. Though the machinery around him seemed mostly to be made of metal Carroll had the disturbing feeling that he was walking amidst the remains of some huge and savagely mutilated beast.

At length he came to and passed the massive engine, then followed the path of an unlikely sized cable to the ship. When he finally passed the sheared off end of the cable, which exposed its hollow silvered interior, he turned to his left and walked along in the ship's shadow. Here there was little wreckage and he could not see the exposed ribs above. The mass of wreckage he had passed previously he surmised to be some part of the ship that had come down separately and perhaps with greater force. Here all he could see that might have been damage was irregularities in the vertical curve of the ship's hull, almost as if in places it had collapsed under its own weight, or supporting struts and rib beams inside had bent or broken.

There were no portals or windows of any kind, as far as Carroll could see, just the curving grey mass of the hull reaching to a height he estimated to be easily more than half a mile. The further he got from the end of the cable the more he comprehended the sheer scale of the ship, and as a consequence realized how he did not comprehend the scale of the construction it rested on. *A folly of gods*, he thought, and pursued the thought no further.

The hull of the ship curved round and after walking many miles he eventually found himself on the other side of it. If there had been some kind of nose cone he had not seen it, and as yet he had no idea of its overall shape. If there had been some change in the curve he had been following he had not seen that either. All he had seen was the grey mass of the hull looming above him with indifferent immensity and all he noticed was his change in position in relation to the sun and the shadows cast.

Eventually he came to another engine, connected to the ship by a massive strut, and held perhaps two hundred feet from the ground. As he walked underneath it he tried to compare it to walking under the wing of a Boeing. It did not compare. The engine itself was bigger than such an aircraft and the strut could have been used as a runway. It seemed to Carroll that it took a very long time to walk from under it, all the while trying not to think of the millions of tons poised above him. No Earthly experience was the same. Humankind just did not build on this scale.

Beyond the engine he come to where more wreckage was strewn from a rent in the grey skin of the ship. Here the rib beams lay exposed and the skin belled out as if from some internal explosion. At length Carroll came to a point where the rent reached to the ground, and he entered the ship.

Once inside Carroll had little choice as to the direction he took because there were few ways through the tangle of machinery through which he could worm. He climbed up and in as if into a tree as he negotiated the dense tangle of beams, tubes, and wires.

Massive cylinders and organ-shaped lumps of metal were everywhere he climbed and coloured crystal sliced his hands like glass. It was like climbing through some strange nightmarish junkyard, and he wondered perhaps if he had made the right choice, to enter the ship. At length he came to a cathedral sized, heart-shaped chamber from which numerous tunnels branched. The floor was curved more acutely than the walls and as he entered he slipped and slid down a metal slope to the centre of the chamber. After inspecting the friction burns on his hands and swearing he stood up and looked around.

The walls of the chamber were of what appeared to Carroll like concrete reinforcing grids layered in no apparent order. The ceiling and floor though were just plain hemispheres of metal, the same metal used to fashion the branching tunnels. To Carroll the chamber looked like some kind of gigantic filter, but to filter what? Fuel? Lubricant? He doubted somehow that this ship was so primitive as to require fuel that needed to be filtered or to require lubricants. But then, what did he know? This chamber, like the scattered wreckage and the huge engines outside, was beyond his apprehension at that moment. He studied the dark maws of the tunnels wondering which one might lead him to those requisites of survival the Clown had mentioned. At random he chose one, entered, and was swallowed by darkness.

The ship was seemingly unending, and what was impressed on Carroll now more than ever before, was the sure knowledge that nothing here had been designed for anything resembling the human form. There were no floors intentionally designed for a man to walk upon, no stairs, and no rooms of a comfortable human scale. Carroll felt like an ant lost in the workings of an aeroplane engine. Had there been power there, had the ship been in working order, he suspected his lifespan would have been as long as the ant's. It occurred to him, as he groped from darkness to twilight and back into darkness, that somewhere there might be some kind of control centre, though he would not have betted on this. With this in mind he directed his search accordingly, always moving to the larger passages, and ever upwards.

Eventually he became too tired to go on. Without food his energy reserves were becoming badly depleted. In semi dark he sat down on one of the cylinders that protruded from a ledge he had been negotiating and from there peered down into a pit of shadow. After a moment he leant back against outwardly curving rods of a glasslike substance and closed his eyes, and it was some time before he opened them again.

As he awoke Carroll became aware of extreme discomfort. In half sleep he could not make up his mind whether it was cold of just his uncomfortable position. Coming fully awake he realized his bladder was protesting. He stood and moved sluggishly to the edge of the pit and there relieved himself into the shadows. It was a moment before he saw that in those shadows, just beyond where he lost sight of his stream of urine, something the size of an elephant had begun shifting.

'Oh hell,' he said softly as he did up his fly and stepped back from the edge. It occurred to him that he would rather not annoy something of that size and that urinating on it was probably not a good move.

Noises began to issue from the pit, noises as of relays closing and electric motors starting up. Carroll shrank back against the wall of glass rods as red and orange glows lit up the surrounding area. Then something began to rise.

The red and orange lights were part of it, a small part. It looked like a mass of scrap metal pressed into a huge ball: cylinders, boxes, and the ubiquitous organ-shaped components, all bound together with segmented tubes that seemed to writhe in the changes of light and shade. It also possessed metallic claws and pincers that waved aimlessly in the air or snapped at phantoms, and other insect shapes on its surface that Carroll was sure were moving, and which made his skin crawl.

'It will not kill you.'

Carroll looked round at the spectral figure of the Clown floating, luminously, only a short distance from him.

'Surprise, surprise,' said Carroll dryly, 'don't you just love surprises.'

'I had expected you to wait outside the ship,' said the Clown.

'Then you misjudged my spirit of adventure and my boredom threshold.' Carroll returned his attention to the robot. 'You see, I get bored waiting around for you to tell me what to do next.'

'I am pushing our enemies from every side, leaving them false trails and giving them the false hope that they might have undermined any plans I have laid. Hopefully they will be unprepared when we really do strike.'

'Yeah,' Carroll's interest was inversely proportional to his physical discomfort, 'and what part do I play, or rather when do I get to play my part?'

'You will see,' said the Clown cryptically, 'for now you must follow this robot. I will return when you have reached your destination.' And with that the Clown receded as if into distance and was gone.

Humming and throbbing the robot rose and moved to the left. Carroll was exhausted, hungry, and thirsty, and even though he was beginning to doubt the Clown's motives for directing him to this place he could do little other than follow the instructions he was given. With a desultory frown he followed the robot, scrambling along the edge while the robot floated through the air with annoying ease. After a short time the robot led him to a slightly spiralling hexagonal section of pipe, and there Carroll hesitated when it followed the pipe up into darkness. A sudden tired and desperate recklessness came over him. Abruptly he ran up the pipe until he was opposite the robot, searched for handholds then jumped. The robot did little more than jerk, then hum as its motors corrected for the extra weight, and continue on its way.

For a moment Carroll just hung in place with his eyes closed, gasping for breath. Movement under his cheek made him open his eyes in trepidation. He had forgotten about the insect shapes. Close to he saw metal antlike bodies joined by tubes or wires ranging from an inch in diameter to the thickness of a hair. These creature things, like the large segmented tubes he clung to, seemed to be holding the robot together. In fact it looked to Carroll like the robot was a huge mobile colony, a swarm. Shivering with phobia Carroll hauled himself up to a more secure position and tried not to think about what was underneath him.

His steady and unworldly mount took Carroll onwards through the nightmarish interior of the ship, and perhaps because it knew his position, it took him by ways he knew he could not have negotiated on foot. It took him through gradually larger and larger spaces so that at times there was nothing visible all around him. It took him past machines of unknown purpose – strange, troubling machines. It took him past structural members like gigantic bones, or trees, he could not make up his mind . And it brought him at last to a vast, spherical, ribbed and blue-lit chamber, where it set him down in the wreckage below two enormous opposed constructions like the business ends of a spot welder.

The two structures rose above him like prehistoric megaliths, yet it seemed likely to Carroll, from all that he had learnt, that these things had been constructed long before the human race could have been said to have existed. He stepped from the settled robot and stumbled on the wreckage which made him inspect it more closely. He saw that it was of the same strange broken machinery he had seen outside the ship, only this wreckage had been exposed to extreme heat and lay in solid masses, fused to the floor. It was not this that held his attention though. Lying amongst the fused machinery were bones, real bones, not part of the weird structure or machinery of the ship, a whole skeleton in fact. *An alien skeleton.*

Carroll knew enough about anatomy to recognize that no Earth-born creature would have a skeleton like this. It was vaguely mammalian, but there was also something of an insect's exoskeleton about it. On closer inspection he could tell that some of the bones had contained organs, like a skull does, only these *bones* bore no resemblance to skulls. The only bones he could see that bore any resemblance to anything he knew were what looked like dinosaur's vertebrae, and ribs forming a three cavity body like a trilobite's. He stooped to pick up one of the vertebrae. It was as light as cobwebs and crumbled to dust in his hand.

For a moment Carroll just stared, allowing the flaky dust to sift through his fingers. The he stood and turned away from the skeleton. Its alien form made him uneasy, and he had more immediate concerns such as thirst and hunger. With the desultory attitude of someone at the limit of his physical resources he wandered round the chamber in search of water. He found none and at length sank down in a fugue by one of the megaliths. Eventually the Clown reappeared.

'Jason Carroll–' began the Clown, but Carroll interrupted.

'If I don't get something to drink then something to eat, soon, I will die... then what of all your plans for me? Or was that the plan?' he rasped, his swollen tongue clicking against the roof of his mouth.

The Clown turned and walked to the robot, the apparent motion of his legs bearing no relation to his forwards progress. At his approach the robot rose up into the air to hover, expectantly. From the Clown, and from the air all around him, issued a multi-toned moaning, clicking, and buzzing. When the sounds finally ceased the robot rose further, then, at unexpected speed, shot up across then out of the chamber.

'It will return shortly with what you require. It will also scan your–' The Clown did not finish. Once again he was abruptly missing.

Carroll sat back against a piece of wreckage. What the Hell is going on? He wondered irritably. What was the Clown up to now? He tried to piece together the course of events and make sense out of them.

First, the Clown had contacted him via his dreams then approached when he was well into the game and near its centre. From this he surmised that he had been one of many. This would account for Ramses' reaction when he had mentioned the

Clown. Was it because he was the closest to winning that he had been chosen for what the Clown required? He thought on that a moment. No, no ... the Clown had told him he had been chosen for his ... abilities... Perhaps all the fighters had had dreams about a Clown. What was it he wondered that he could do that the Clown and all his machines could not? He had no idea. It was difficult to think with his tongue swollen in his mouth and his body crying out for liquid. He looked up anxiously for the robot.

The robot eventually returned with a metallic, kidney-shaped bladder in one of its claw manipulators. Tubes depended from this as from a real kidney, and from the ragged end of one of these water spilled. Carroll lurched to his feet and had his hands on the bladder before the robot had even landed. He drank deep once the bladder was released to him. Nothing could have tasted more delicious than the bitter metallic water. It was cool on his chapped lips, trickled soothingly past his ceramic tongue, and thawed the sore dryness of his throat.

After a few minutes he had sated his thirst and took another package proffered to him by the robot. Wrapped in a nacreous sheet of some silky fabric the content of the package contained was not easy to identify. It was about the size and shape of a slice of bread, had a fibrous, puttylike consistency and smelt of brewer's yeast and oranges. After a moment Carroll remembered where he had smelt something similar to this. The substance smelt just like multi-vitamin tablets. He assumed it must be food and took a bite. Immediately his mouth was awash with saliva and before he knew it he had eaten half of the slab. By an act of will he stopped eating and drank some more water, then he waited to see if he was going to vomit, not because he thought the food might be poisonous, but because he did not know if his stomach could handle it after being so long without solids. Then, when everything seemed to be fine, he ate the rest.

While Carroll sated his hunger and thirst the robot rested before him with its lights flickering to the promptings of hidden thoughts. Eventually, as if coming to a decision, it rose into the air. Carroll watched it go without much interest, then he found the most comfortable spot he could amongst the wreckage, and was soon asleep.

Chapter Eight

He was in Northern Ireland. There were snipers. That was the main thing he remembered, though he was sure he had been involved in an intricate situation beforehand that explained their presence. Coming out of the tight bowel-clenching fear of physical injury, he became aware that he was dreaming and that the staccato rattling he was hearing was not from automatic weapons, but from something near to where he slept. He then woke fully.

The chamber was lit now with a soft blue radiance issuing from no discernible source. Wiping the sleep from his eyes Carroll saw that the robot had returned and was the source of the noise. With its many manipulators and tool-bearing appendages it was working on a machine that had not been present when Carroll had fallen asleep. The machine looked something like a creation booth, something like a resurrection machine, and a lot like a water tank with a door in it.

Yawning and still rubbing at his eyes, Carroll stood and approached to watch the work in progress. Abruptly he had to jerk away as an arc welder flashed and sprayed the floor with molten globules. It was a moment before his sight returned, and when it did he realized that the robot had ceased to work.

'Warning given time weld unshielded next,' said the robot in a voice that was a combination of Carroll's and the Clown's. Blinking with surprise Carroll saw that the voice issued from a new addition to its chaotic structure. Held, seemingly at random by the insect shapes, was a metal copy of the human speech making apparatus from lungs to lips, either side of which were ears. Carroll had seen some strange things lately but this was the most Daliesque.

'What is that you are working on?' Carroll asked, as the robot set too again.

Without slowing the robot explained, 'Fractal entachyon multiplier ... now the power feed...now–'

'No, everything, the entire machine,' said Carroll, realizing the robot was taking him too literally.

A long pause ensued before the robot replied, 'Life form viewpoint understood. This is a creation booth.'

'Is it for me? Is it to provide me with the necessities of life?' He was not actually thinking of those necessities. He was thinking that perhaps this machine would not be as limited as the one the Reaper had provided. It was a lot larger and more complex than the ones back there.

'Yes, partially,' replied the robot.

Carroll moved forward with studied nonchalance to inspect the booth. Like the resurrection machine on top of the cliff it had a pedestal mounted control console. The controls were beyond him. He swore quietly before again addressing the robot.

'How will I operate it?' he asked.

'Creation booth through me–' the robot began and then corrected, 'The creation booth is voice-operated through me.' Then, 'This creation booth will be voice-operated through me.'

Carroll was impressed by the robots improvement in the use of English though disheartened by its reply.

'How long until it's ready,' he asked.

'Approximately four minutes once welding recommences.'

'I'll leave you to it then,' said Carroll with irony.

After a relay clicking pause the robot continued its task. Carroll walked away aimlessly but eventually found himself standing by the skeleton. After staring for a while he decided that it seemed less alien to him now, less frightening, perhaps because he now felt more capable and hence more optimistic. In his mind he now found he was able piece the bits of it back together and speculate as to what the original creature might have looked like, and decided it was not one he would have wanted to meet in a dark alley. He pushed his hands in his pockets and turned away.

The robot had finished by the time Carroll returned to it, and was resting silently beside the creation booth. He noticed the number of cables connecting it to the booth, and decided to try something.

'The creation booth is ready then?'

The robot did not reply, so he rephrased his words as a question, realizing that the robot had taken them as a statement. 'Is this creation booth ready to be used now?' he asked.

'Yes,' replied the robot succinctly.

'Tell me again how I use it.'

'To use this creation booth you tell me what you require and I convert your request into machine language.'

'What range of goods will this booth create?'

'Any inanimate object on existence on Earth up to the time of your death, and able to fit within this booth.'

'Nothing is proscribed?'

The machine was silent.

'In that case,' said Carroll with satisfaction, 'I'll have an M1 assault rifle with two thirty-round magazines loaded alternately with armoured and mercury tipped bullets.'

Lights flickered and the robot and the creation booth hummed with a surge of energy. Carroll moved forward when the door thunked open to show his order had been filled. It was new. It even had packing grease on it. He picked it up and rapidly checked it over, loaded a magazine, pointed at the far wall of the chamber, and fire. The vicious staccato rattling was the best sound he had heard in a long time. Contemplatively he next ordered a twelve inch pizza with anchovies and a four-pack of Ruddles County. After eating and drinking he really got to work. When the Clown came he was seated on the floor bolting a laser-spot sight on the M1 and was surrounded by mortars, armour-piercing missiles, hand guns and ammunition.

'This is why I chose you, and I am pleased I did, now,' was the first thing the Clown said. Carroll looked up – a child disturbed while playing with his favourite toys.

'Pleased? Why are you pleased?'

'Your familiarity with modern Earth weaponry. These machines,' he gestured with a spectral arm at the creation booth, 'are controlled by a central information bank and are limited by the invention of the people of Earth. I made them that way, and here and now it is difficult to make them any other. And only now, since the advent of your twentieth century, have there been weapons that can be effective against the Four.'

Carroll laid the assault rifle tenderly across his lap.

'What is it you want me to do again?' he asked with a faint smile.

'I want you to steal my soul disc and bring it back here,' replied the Clown.

Carroll gazed at the weaponry that surrounded him. It seemed he would get a chance to use it. His smile turned into a grin.

♠♠♠

'Perhaps now would be a good time for you to tell me more about the Four. I'll need to know their weaknesses, and their strengths,' said Carroll.

'Hopefully you will need to know no more than you know at present. The element of surprise ... a lightning raid ... these clichés apply. It would be best for you to go in as quickly as you can, when the moment is right, destroying anything in your way. You then retrieve my soul disc and return with it here as quickly as you can.'

Carroll bowed his head for a minute then said, 'Transport?'

'To the point!' replied the Clown, 'this way,' and with that strange floating gait led Carroll from the chamber to a place in the ship like the upper reaches of a jungle, only the branches here were pipes, ducts and hanging wires. Carroll had to climb through this tangle like the denizen of a jungle, the Clown floating mockingly before him, until at length he reached a place where two massive ribbed ducts ran at thirty degrees up into a darkness where leaf-like shapes could just be discerned.

'There,' said the Clown, pointing with a wavering arm, then he led Carroll up the chancy ducts to the first shape.

The closer he got to it the more Carroll thought it looked like a huge beech leaf. It was even joined by a little stem to the duct. Standing over it at last he saw it looked so much like a leaf that the similarity could not have been accidental. Unlike a leaf, though, it was forty feet long and thirty wide.

'This is your transport,' stated the Clown. Carroll stared at him incredulously as he continued, 'It flies, and with very little practise you will learn how to fly it. It is silent and its speed is governed by how well you can hold on. It can also serve as a weapons platform. In practical terms it is indestructible and there is no limit to the weight it can carry.'

Practical terms? Thought Carroll as he stepped onto the craft. Much to his surprise it did not waver under his weight.

'A leaf?' he said looking around distractedly.

'A conceit of mine,' said the Clown, 'this is the shape I predicted certain forms of life would take to utilise the sun's energy.'

'You were right,' said Carroll, too shell-shocked to doubt.

'It is not often that I am wrong,' said the Clown matter-of-factly, before going on to instruct Carroll on how to detach the craft from the duct. Not thinking too much about what he was doing Carroll followed those instructions. Only when the stem detached from its anchor point did it occur to him that it was attached to nothing, and he clung to the edge in sudden fear. The craft did not even quiver though. It remained motionless relative to the duct. After a moment Carroll stood up and glanced sheepishly to the Clown, who then instructed him on how to steer the craft.

The stem folded up into a joystick and changed the direction of the craft on the horizontal plane. Indentations in the end of it controlled the height of the craft. Shortly, standing like some pixie scooter driver, Carroll was negotiating the craft through the metalled jungle.

♠♠♠

'What will I face back there? What is the situation at present?'

'During the time you were escaping I was keeping the Four busy–'

'Three,' corrected Carroll, without thinking.

'No, four. The Reaper is still extant. They are able to resurrect themselves.' The Clown pause while Carroll took this in then went on, 'They are not aware that you still live. They think that you are permanently dead. When Anubis saw you he swiftly destroyed the machine you were in unaware that in that moment it transported you elsewhere. In the information banks I made what he believed appear to be that case.'

'So now things are back the way they were before, they're still playing the game?'

'No. they are aware that I have made a move. They think they have negated this move, but they are not sure and are still wary. I have been attempting to direct their attention away from the things that most concern me.'

'It seems you hardly need my help... but you still have not answered my original question.'

'When the time comes for you to steal my soul disc I am not sure precisely what you will find at the game board. One thing is certain though. You will not encounter the Four.'

'Why not?'

'At present they are one AU, you know this measurement?' Carroll shook his head. 'They are approximately ninety million miles to spin-ward destroying an installation I caused to be built a thousand years ago. As they return from this I will cause another diversion which they will think to be the main event.'

'You believe in forward planning then,' said Carroll wryly, then fell silent while he negotiated the craft round a particularly difficult tangle of pipes and wires, before going on, 'What if they take the disc with them?'

'This the one thing I can be sure they will not do. The place where it is kept is where they have agreed to keep it. Not one of them would trust one of the others to carry the disc. Their distrust of each other is equal to their hate.'

88

'Ah,' said Carroll, as if he understood, then he fell silent again as another tangle had to be negotiated round.

The Clown continued talking once they were past. 'You wondered why I need your help, Jason Carroll. The reason is simply speed, and information. To the Four you no longer exist, also you are capable of independent action. I could not send a robot because all my robots are connected to the main information banks and should the Four become aware of them they would be immediately shut down. They cannot shut you down without direct action, and you can move fast enough to get this task done before they return.'

'Very ego inflating,' said Carroll, 'what happens when I get the disc back here?'

'I cannot destroy the Four completely, that is, prevent them from being resurrected, without being physically present. You see, once physically present again I will be in control of the information banks – in control of all that happens on the disc.'

With all that they revealed and all that Carroll felt they hid he felt an unearthly chill at those words.

'What is the point of the game?' he asked after a while.

'What is the point of any game?' was the Clown's reply.

'The Four are robots. You said...'

'The Four are robots, but robots more complex than organic carbon life. And they are insane in their own terms and in any terms you would care to name.'

'They have emotions?'

'Yes, the prime of which is hate. The only things they hate more than me are themselves.'

'Why?'

'They hate what they perceive as the purposelessness of their existence and hate their inability to end it, in each other and in themselves.'

'That still doesn't explain the game. I cannot accept that it is totally pointless.'

'The game is their vengeance upon me for creating them. When they captured my life field in my soul disc they were aware that I could not be totally confined. What you see before you is my ghost, in a shape forced upon me by them... They also found a way I could be forced back into my soul disc for limited periods of time. Their vengeance is the way of that banishment. Every time my soul disc is struck I am made aware of the suffering that led up to it being struck, of the petty waste, and of the fact that my greatest project is stalled at the brink of completion.'

Carroll said, 'If they hate themselves more than you why don't they destroy themselves?'

'Perhaps because they know that if they do I would eventually win my way to freedom again. Or perhaps they are in the process of destroying themselves now. I sometimes think that there are loop holes in my confinement for good reasons.'

'A death wish?'

'Perhaps...'

When Carroll landed the leaf craft back by the creation booth the Clown abandoned him once again to provide distractions for the Four. While he was gone Carroll ordered a further large quantity of equipment through the booth, then with the assistance of the robot, mounted that equipment on the craft. When he had finished there were four Browning M2s fixed to point down from the craft at forty five degrees, four rocket launchers, with flame baffles behind them, pointing down at the same angle, a chair fixed by the joystick with controls from which these weapons could be fired and many other hand weapons within reach. The Clown visited him twice while he was working. The first time was only a short visit because he was dispelled by the ringing of his soul disc. The second time was to tell Carroll that the Four were suspicious of his diversions and readying to return.

'I'll move now then,' Carroll replied, and then turned to the pile of equipment he had recently acquired from the booth: a pair of binoculars, a well-padded flying suit, and a helmet with visor and gloves. He donned the clothing, hung the binoculars round his neck, boarded his vessel and took it up off the ground.

The Clown led him, quite swiftly, out into the light of the eternal sunset, and even this made his eyes smart. He had forgotten how much colour there was, even here. He had forgotten how far it was possible to see. Like leashed hounds his eyes strained towards the distance.

'This diversion ... I presume it is ready,' said Carroll.

'Yes,' said the Clown, who now appeared to be seated against one of the gun mountings. 'If I understand my creations well enough this will draw them away.'

'Well?' asked Carroll, 'what exactly is the plan, or is there a plan?'

'There is a plan,' said the Clown after a lengthy pause.

'You will return to the Reaper's base and await my diversion. Once it has occurred you will probably see the Four returning. Wait for them to be drawn off then go in. Once you have possession of my–' A distant discordant ringing caused the Clown's form to shimmer, crack, and then fly apart. Long inured to this now Carroll continued on towards the steel cliff.

♠♠♠

The craft rose up the face of the cliff with no problems. It was Carroll who had the problems. Once at the top of the cliff he found himself panting, and his ears adjusted to the change in pressure with a sound like a gunshot. By the time he had found the fused remains of the resurrection machine his breathing had returned to normal and other ill effects were minimal.

Carroll had decided long before that given the opportunity he would come back here to confirm or deny a suspicion. Bringing the craft to a halt above the machine he saw that his suspicions were confirmed. Amidst the fused and distorted metal lay the charred corpse of a man in combat clothing.

♠♠♠

Carroll had been killed here and resurrected at the bottom of the cliff. He wondered then if he had been killed in Anubis's attack or if he had sacrificed his life the moment he had placed his soul disc in the console. Whatever, this proved that the Clown was prepared to lie. He resolved to distrust the Clown as much as he could without being totally uncooperative. He sent the leaf craft on its way.

Chapter Nine

The journey from the wrecked machine to the Reaper's base seemed incredibly short compared to the last time he had made the trip. After crossing the featureless expanse he came in low and cautiously. What he saw when he finally landed next to the mirror glass building made him sick to the stomach.

After being resurrected and perhaps before moving on with its three fellows the Reaper had rid itself of its fighters, perhaps because they were now aware of the possibility of escape, perhaps out of spite. Carroll did not know. All he knew was that to a man they had been burnt. Before the building lay a mass of charred bones, and grey ash that sifted and swirled in recalcitrant breezes.

Carroll stepped from the craft with an Uzi in his hand, and walking as if on the thin ice over a swamp, moved to the door of the building. He would have gone in with stun grenades in the manner he had been trained, but that could not be so. He dreaded to think how far sound would travel here. With care not to step on any broken glass he edged up to the doors. They slid open, but not all the way. Halfway back they jammed with a metallic crunch, closed half and inch, crunched again, then tried to open again. Cursing, Carroll stepped through the gap into to room beyond with his machine pistol sweeping from side to side as he searched the place. The doors only stopped their racket when he moved away from them.

On one of the tables stood a bottle of schnapps and a plate with the remains of pickled herrings on it. Carroll stopped by the table and stirred the remains with the barrel of his Uzi. But for this bottle and this plate there was nothing else on the tables. He moved on through the room to the door at its back, carefully eased open a door and went through, then checked room after room. Kruger tried to jump him in the fifth room.

He came from behind the door with a bottle held high. It was the first place Carroll checked and he had the SS officer cold for a good two seconds. Kruger kept coming though. At the last moment, Carroll eased off on the trigger, and drop-kicked him in the stomach. Kruger went down puking herrings and schnapps.

'Do not kill me! Do not kill me!'

Carroll simply stood over him wondering if painful death had made him like this or if he had always been like it.

'I won't kill you just yet,' said Carroll. 'Stand up.'

Kruger eased himself carefully to his feet, flinching every time Carroll moved. Carroll nodded to the door and with Kruger led the way out into the main room.

'Sit down.'

Kruger sat, and Carroll sat opposite him.

'What happened here then. Why are you still alive?'

'It is not my fault.'

Carroll raised the Uzi higher and pointed it at Kruger's face. 'I asked you a question.'

Quickly Kruger replied, 'After you ran four of the others ran as well. They went in different directions. The rest stayed here. Sometime after that, I do not know how long, another Reaper came. He called me forwards and made me collect all his coins ... from the ground ... I think they are connected to us, for he selected four of them and ... I think he burnt the four who had escaped. He then called all who remained outside. They all came thinking it was another game. Then, while I stood by his throne he burnt all the others. I could do nothing. He said I was to become his General. Then he left. I do not want to be his General.'

Carroll nodded then stood up. Kruger watched him like a pheasant watching a fox, his face white and beaded with sweat. Carroll stared outside at the ash and bones. Dispensed with, simply dispensed with. He wondered what it would mean for Kruger to become the Reaper's General. Would he be made into a machine? He turned back to Kruger.

'What happened to the discs? Did he take them with him?'

Kruger glanced outside. 'No. He cast them on the ground again and told me to collect them up in readiness for his return. He also told me to clear up all the ash and bones and load it in sacks...'

A small rebellion, Carroll decided, but then what right did he have to judge? Put in the same position could he have down any different? Yes, because he would not have put himself in that position by betraying his fellows. Perhaps it was too harsh a judgement, but Carroll decided to keep to it. He gazed at Kruger expressionlessly.

'I will give you five minutes. If I can still see you after that time I will kill you.'

Kruger did not hesitate. He leapt up and was out of the doors in moments. Carroll followed him outside and watched him fleeing towards the sun. After five minutes he was still in sight but Carroll did not shoot at him. He knew what awaited him out there and a bullet would have been a kindness. Carroll did not feel very kind. He returned to the building.

The place was empty of life now and Carroll allowed himself to relax. Dispelling Kruger from his thoughts, he took some tools from the craft and set about removing a partition from the wall. His task was not difficult as the building was of flimsy construction. Once he had removed it he went out to the craft and brought that inside. He then leant the partition back in place. With this done he went on to do the one other task he had set himself to do before he settled down to wait.

They were strewn all around where he had thought he had destroyed the Reaper' soul discs, about twenty of them. Taking care not to miss any of them amongst the wreckage of this Reaper and this General, he collected them all up and weighed them in the palm of his hand. *Like poker chips,* he thought – the lives of twenty men. *Which ones?* He wondered. Which ones were Ellery, Julius, the Masai. Which one was Kruger? They all looked the same to him. He pocketed them and headed back to the building.

Inside he sat at the table where he, Ellery and Julius had played cards, while lumps of explosive had sweated nitro-glycerine in their pockets. He unpacked the supplies he had brought from the ship, as he dared not use his creation booth here, and he ate a meal he didn't taste, then smoked, but even the cigarettes were tasteless. In time the Clown's diversion began.

It started as a barely discernible humming that built in intensity and power. Aware that this must be what he had been waiting for, Carroll stood and went to his craft. As he strapped himself in the humming became a resonant vibration. Chairs and tables began to rattle and tableware to crash upon the floor. Carroll moved his craft to where he had laid the panel back in place, and peering out through the jammed doors he saw five specks hurtling across the sky. Flashes of red light ignited the sky and one of the specks fell. The others continued on, sunward. Once they were out of sight Carroll eased his craft forwards pushing the panel over. Soon he was outside and able rise above the building and look around.

The specks, he guessed, were the Four, heading towards the Clown's ship. He had no ideas about the one that had fallen. Now was his time to move. A slight pressure in one of the indentations of the joystick and a forward pressure took him up at forty-five degrees at an acceleration that sucked his eyeballs towards his mouth. At a height of fifty feet he looked towards the sun and suffered a stomach turning disorientation. The sun seemed to have moved, and it took him a moment to dispel the illusion.

The Clown had told him that the steel plain was a gigantic matter converter – a tool used for the building of the solar disc, and by the way he had said it Carroll guessed it was not a permanent fixture. That must be what was happening: the Clown was moving the steel plain. Carroll slammed the joystick forwards. He had things to do.

The hexagons sped underneath him and for a time he felt as if he were flying high over a patchwork of fields in England. Soon he caught sight of the mount he had fought his way to the top of. It looked like an ants nest, a termite's hill, but those were people down there. But as far as he could see no game was in progress, no pillars of smoke were visible, so what were they doing?

He came in low over the top of the mount and saw that the people were gathered closer around it. Closer, and he saw that they were all armed and that a number of them had gathered in a cordon around the Clown's soul disc. These men, fifteen of them in all, were armed with what looked like three-foot long toothpicks. In a gout of smoke ruby light flashed on his arm. With a flick of his wrist Carroll sent the craft high into the air with red light flashing and splashing ineffectually against its underside. He then sent it hurtling away from the mount until the firing stopped. Tearing open the fabric of his shirt he peered at a pencil-sized hole cut and cauterised through his left bicep.

His arm felt stiff but hardly hurt at all. *Adrenalin,* he decided – it would hurt later on, if he was still alive.

The men had obviously been placed there as a precaution. It was not their fault. They could not be blamed for not knowing he was seeking to end the game. *They can be resurrected though*, he rationalized, and turned his craft back towards the mount.

On his first pass he flew high and slow above the mount, the bottom of the craft continuously being struck with laser fire. He turned and circled and, with his arm beginning to ache, clumsily dropped CS gas canisters over the side to confuse matters below. Once all these were gone, he moved the craft aside to let it cool, watching as the mount became shrouded in tear gas cut through with random stabs of red light like needles in cotton wool. They couldn't see him now, it seemed.

With his left hand resting on the controls that fired his missile launchers and machine guns he came in low over to one side of the cloud of tear gas, and opened fire with the guns on one side of his craft. No single shot could be heard – the sound like that of a wave hitting a shingle beach, only much amplified. As the belts chattered through cartridge cases swamped the deck and rattled off the side. The sound of the missiles going seemed like the concerted hiss of a disturbed snake pit.

Two explosions lit the cloud of tear gas, roughly on either side of the top of the mount. Carroll knew that the soul disc was indestructible but did not want to blow it from its position there. It would be rather stupid to go through all this and then be unable to find the damned thing. He next turned his craft and ran through the same routine with the machine guns and missile launchers on that side. Finally, when there was nothing left to fire, he donned a gas mask and spiralled his craft down into the smoke.

Those shooting at him from below had ceased to do so either because they could no longer see him, or because there was no one below to shoot at him. In moments he found the top hexagon and came in to land. Moans and screams issued from the smoke all around, but he ignored them. This was the business he had been in all his life. All around the craft lay bodies peppered with bullets, but he took no chances, climbing from his craft with his Uzi in his good hand and grenades on his belt.

The Clown's soul disc was difficult to locate in the smoke. Twice he nearly stepped off of the edge of the hexagon and innumerable times he slipped in blood and stumbled over corpses. Eventually it loomed out of the smoke at him, swaying in its contorted silver frame. At the foot of it, like bloody offerings, lay two men, still clutching their laser weapons to their mutilated bodies. Carroll stepped over them and tugged at the clasps that held the disc in place, then he whirled around when he thought he saw a shadow moving through the smoke. No shadow. He turned back to the disc and inspected the clasps, which were supported by thin chains. He put the barrel of the Uzi against one of the chains and squeezed off a shot. The chain parted and the disc fell against its support and tolled like a doom bell.

Carroll holstered his Uzi then yanked the chain from where it had been fed through the frame. The disc came free and fell against his leg. He swore. It weighed about as much as a car wheel. He began rolling it back towards his craft thinking it might make a suitable wheel for some chariot of fire.

Ahead of him, the now thinning smoke was lit by a flash of red. A laser firing, but not towards him. He halted, lowered

99

the disc to the ground, and drew his Uzi. The sounds of abrupt movement impinged. He waited, sweat running like ants through his hair. Finally he decided he could wait no longer, since the Four were probably on their way back even now. He unhooked a grenade from his belt, pulled its pin, and tossed it ahead of him, then crouched down using the Clown's soul disc as a shield. The detonation was sharp and powerful; a bright flash lighting the smoke before brushing it aside. Carroll stood in time to see the deadly scene before him.

The android with blind eyes was running towards him at phenomenal speed. In no way could this one have been mistaken for the man Carroll had fought and killed. This was the machine that had taken his head off with his own sword. It was not his only worry either. Off to one side, two men were levelling lasers in his general direction. He lifted his Uzi and fired as he dived to one side. The shots thwacked into the android but to no effect. Carroll dropped his Uzi, groping for a grenade. Suddenly the android became blackly silhouetted against this flare of red. Hissing, bubbling and boiling smoke the android flew in half along a line from its shoulder to its groin, showing sparks, cogs, and metallic bones all about.

Carroll pushed himself upright and watched in stunned amazement as a pair of legs kicked round in circles like an unwinding clockwork toy. He gazed at the metal skull attached to a shoulder and arm, the fingers of the hand still flexing. Then he looked up from these macabre debris to the two Egyptians striding towards him.

'He thought us naive enough to believe this part of the game. We allowed him to think that,' said one of them.

Carroll thought he recognized the manner of speech even though translated, and was not surprised when a passing band of smoke finally revealed Ramses.

100

'Anubis?' Carroll asked, standing up and removing his gas mask.

The two Egyptians came to halt before him, their eyes streaming but their expressions determined. For a moment he could not tell them apart until Ramses spoke again.

'I will have my treasure and my slaves yet,' he said, his eyes locking with Carroll's. Then he and the other Egyptian stooped down, took up the Clown's soul disc and carried it to the craft. No more was said for a moment, and Carroll, acting as vanguard, saw no further movement in the smoke. Once they had loaded the disc Carroll stepped aboard and strapped in before turning to Ramses and his twin.

'Thank you,' he said.

Ramses reply was, 'Serve Osiris well soldier. I would burn no more.'

Carroll nodded in understanding and with no more to say took his vessel up and out of the smoke. It could have been his imagination, but as he came up into clear air he thought he heard a wild yell, and he thought he saw two flashes of red.

Once up and out of the smoke Carroll sent his craft speeding in the direction of the Reaper's old base again. He could not return directly to the ship with the Four likely returning from there. All he could now do was go into hiding and await further instructions from the Clown, or until he knew for certain it was safe to return to the ship. And so he flew on, continually searching the sky for the four black specks that would mean failure and death for him. It seemed to take forever for the building to come into sight, but eventually it did. Gratefully he spiralled the craft down and taxied it within.

As soon as the craft settled to the floor Carroll opened up the medical kit he had brought along, since his arm was beginning to hurt rather badly now. He first injected a heavy dose of local anaesthetic, then he packed the plasma-seeping wound with cotton wool soaked in an antiseptic and bound it up tightly. By the time he had finished dressing it his arm was going dead and hung like something separate from him. He made a sling to support it then quickly moved to the partition and wrestled it into place.

Now as safe as he could be he went to inspect his cargo. It was, as he had thought from his first glimpse of it, just like a huge coloured CD. However, it was not made from plastic but the same material as the other discs – translucent and red and the texture of glass. It was a yard across, an inch thick, and had a hole at its centre an inch in diameter. Gazing at this recording of fantastic life, this prison, Carroll wondered not for the first or last time about the Clown. He took his own disc from his pocket and pressed it against the Clown's disc. These things were made from a single information-carrying molecule, the Clown had told him. What information makes me what I am? All he knew and all he had experienced, was part of it, obviously. But he realized that stored on this disc must be the blue-prints for his body.

Carroll leant back against a table and flipped his disc like a coin. It was pertinent to remember that the being he would resurrect, of which the Clown was ghost, a mere trace, was older than human history, older in fact than the planet the human race had evolved on. The Clown was a being capable of engineering a construction beyond the ability of the human mind to comprehend. And, shortly, he, Jason Carroll, would resurrect it. He flipped his disc again and pocketed it, wondering if he would regret what he intended to do. Four black shapes crossing the sky visible beyond the doors reminded him that he had few choices really.

'Are you ready?' came the Clown's voice from behind him.

He turned to view the innocuous spectre. 'How can I be anything else?'

The Clown tilted his head and regarded him for a moment. 'If all goes well, Jason Carroll,' he said, 'you and many others will be free of the Four.'

'Yes, but will I be *free*?' Carroll asked as he climbed into the seat of the craft.

'Define freedom,' said the Clown.

Carroll remained silent as he manoeuvred the craft to the wall partition. As it fell like a drawbridge before him he chuckled. 'That's a difficult one. No one's free, I suppose.' He turned to peered at the Clown, now hovering behind his seat. 'I was just wondering what comes after the Four.'

The Clown replied, 'When the Four are neutralised I shall finish the project I began. This solar disc will be made habitable and the human race will be resurrected to live upon it.'

'Seems almost too good to be true,' said Carroll.

'You do not like happy endings?'

'No, just a pessimist I suppose.'

They flew on, out over the steel plain and its abrupt ending, then out of the landscape of grey and red. Carroll had other questions he could have asked but he felt no inclination. The Clown would have answered him, but he knew he could never be sure of those answers until they were proven true or otherwise. He was tired now; tired of the fantastic and the strange. He wanted events brought to their resolution, to see the Four gone and to know the truth about the Clown. So thinking, he increased their speed towards the ship.

Pillars of smoke again, he thought, when at last the ship came into sight. Then, irrelevantly, *Pillars of Hercules*. Of course, the Four had been here.

'What attracted them here?' he asked.

'The steel plain, as you call it, I shifted by the action of one of the ship's motors. They came here to destroy the motor and the one they thought to be the culprit.' Carroll thought back to the five black specks and the one that fell.

'The robot,' he guessed. The Clown nodded in reply.

Closer to the ship and Carroll saw that the smoke was coming from the fused remains of the massive turbine he had walked under before entering the ship. It was now an empty, holed and sagging husk, sitting in a pool of glass. He thought that a shame.

'How did this motor shift the steel... the matter converter?' he asked.

'It generated a displaced gravity field,' replied the Clown.

'Oh, right,' said Carroll, aware now that perhaps there were some things that could not be explained to him. In silent contemplation of gravity fields and matter converting machines the size of the isle of Wight he brought his craft down to the hole torn in the top of the ship and eventually to the chamber at its heart. Since he had left this place, and until the time of its destruction, it seemed the robot had been very busy.

The wreckage strewn all around those two megalithic constructions no longer looked quite like wreckage. Cables, pipes, and ducts linked fused mass to fused mass. Many areas had been cleared to make way for massive tanks and veined spheres, also linked into the network.

'There,' said the Clown, pointing to an area below the two megaliths. Snapping out of amazed reverie Carroll moved

104

the craft to the area indicated. As he landed he could see what his next task would be.

Below the megaliths lay a lump of machinery like a grounded flying saucer, a ramp from the floor up to the top of it, in which had been made an indentation exactly the size of the Clown's disc. Carroll was already out of his seat and reaching for the disc when the Clown stated the obvious.

'Take my disc up there, and place it where it must go.'

Carroll nodded, and wincing, took the disc under his good arm, two fingers in the conveniently positioned hole, and stepped carefully through the tangle of machinery to the bottom of the ramp. *Am I doing the right thing?* He wondered as he mounted the ramp. *How could he possibly know?* Suddenly such thoughts were far from his mind as a powerful blast rocked the chamber. The Clown, floating ahead of him on the ramp, tilted to look up at the roof of the chamber.

'They detect ... power drain!' the Clown yelled, his voice going in and out of human audibility. Carroll watched the Clown shape before him and truly understood, for the first time, that this was not what he was to resurrect. Another blast shook the chamber, closer this time. Carroll went down on his knees to prevent himself falling from the ramp walk. He knew he had no alternatives. He must do as the Clown bid him.

'Hurr... eey... eey!' came the Clown's distorted shout. As Carroll stumbled to his feet he saw the Clown shape flicker and subliminally become something else before returning to normal.

Another blast rocked the chamber. The ceiling cracked and a boulder-sized chunk of a substance like crystallised resin crashed to the floor and shattered into a thousand broken-flint pieces. Carroll struggled on as the blasts continued with frightening regularity. All he could do...

The resin substance started to rain continuously and nearby fires lit up the chamber as Carroll reached the top of the ramp. It would take him just a moment now to place the disc into its indentation, but he hesitated.

'You took that form for my sake! It was not forced on you!' he shouted at the Clown. 'You lied to me! Is that all you lied about!?'

The Clown's reply was immediate and succinct. 'That is all, but there is much I have not told you.'

'Why?!' Carroll yelled, rolling the disc into position next to the indentation.

'Because my true form would be a nightmare to you. Because there is so much you simply cannot understand.'

Carroll peered up at the cracked ceiling, back at the Clown, then allowed the disc to drop into place. It seemed to hesitate as it fell, but when it finally settled into position the effect was immediate.

Like a coin into a juke box, thought Carroll irreverently as around him the machinery came alive with light, movement, and a low grating hum of unthinkable power. He turned and ran down the ramp, leapt onto his craft, and took it to a relatively safe position at the side of the chamber. And from there he watched a nightmare come to life.

Greenish fluid pulsed from one of the tanks and filled pipes Carroll had taken to be opaque. Some parts of the machinery glowed with heat while other parts frosted as they were super-cooled. Yellow-white, red, and blue lasers flashed at ground level like spider silk, their presence only becoming visible when they speared gusts of steam or coloured vapour. Carroll gaped in awed amazement, aware that all this power was not only directed at the disc. He got the impression that the disc was only a stepping stone to the two megaliths at the centre of the chamber. He watched as cycles of light and power built to a crescendo as the disc turned blinding white hot and the megaliths turned dull red. Then he watched as between the two top opposing faces lightning crackled as if between the fingers of Zeus.

The lightning went on and on, and even though it was leaving lines of blackness across his vision Carroll could not draw his eyes away. Something was happening there, something more than that brute, candent display of power. A three dimensional pattern of bluish light began to form; a pattern like a flaw in a precious stone. And this flaw grew larger and brighter round something solid, something that shifted with feral life.

In the light it moved with the slow, speed belying sinuosity of a snake, its terrible head thrust forwards on a cable strength neck, its lower jaw a slowly extending mandible like a dragon fly larva's, though little else of it could be compared to an insect. None of its sensory apparatus was recognizable to Carroll. There were hollows where eyes might have been, but no eyes. There were tufts of fibre round its mouth parts and rows of nodes along its horse-like face. All these might have been sense organs, but what they were sensing was a mystery to Carroll. He turned away to rest his eyes. It was easy to try and compare aspects of this creature with creatures of Earth, but such comparison missed out on what came over most strongly to him, what he had first felt when seeing what must have been the skeleton of its original body on the floor below. It was alien. It was the product of ecology and evolution other than that of Earth. It was extraneous, not easily amenable to human comprehension. Carroll shuddered and wondered just what he had done.

At length the lightning flashed out, and as if this were a signal the bombardment ceased also. Carroll returned his gaze to the fingers of Zeus and saw that the creature was gone. Then he lowered his gaze to see it standing by its disc. *This is the Clown*, he thought, and had to repress the hysterical laughter that bubbled up in his throat.

The Clown reached down and took up its disc in what might perhaps have been described as a hand. As it did so Carroll reached across and took up a weapon he had not used as yet: a multiple rocket launcher, something in shape like a large version of an old tommy gun, only the circular magazine was a ring with nine missiles on it. The Clown let out a cry that was as alien in its joy as it itself was in appearance. One handed, Carroll aimed the launcher and pulled back and held the trigger. Four missiles sped away on tongues of fire before he lost control of the launcher.

One impacted on what remained of the ceiling of the chamber. The other three struck the black throne that had been silently descending through the hole in that ceiling. The Four had arrived.

Chapter Ten

The green skinned, multi-armed goddess of death blew apart along with her throne. As the recoil threw Carroll back he was gratified to see her burning fragments falling through the air, but falling to the deck of his craft he saw Quetzalcoatl coming through the ceiling on its floating dais, closely followed by the Reaper and Anubis. But they did not head towards him though; the Clown was their main concern.

The moment Carroll had fired the missiles the Clown's head had snapped round to trace their course. As they impacted it moved with unhuman speed and grace. Its limbs became a blur as it shot to one side. Even so the stab of lasers traced its path across the machinery that had resurrected it. Upon reaching the wall its limbs blurred again and the disc emitted a sonic crack as it left its hand. Carroll did not see the disc in flight. All he saw was Quetzalcoatl's dais rip apart and explode, and the feathered serpent falling in two writhing and electrically crackling pieces.

The Clown was gone again as the spot it had been standing in became a molten pool. It went up the curving and completely smooth wall as if it had not heard of gravity. When it reached the level of the Reaper's throne it leapt out from the wall in a flat trajectory. It hit the Reaper's throne hard and fast, knocking it against the edge of the chamber. Pieces of throne fell, shortly followed by dismembered pieces of Reaper. The Clown leapt as a line of red sliced the Reaper's throne in two.

By this time Carroll had retrieved his missile launcher. He fired two missiles. One missed Anubis and streaked off through the hole in the ceiling to explode somewhere else in the ship. The other exploded behind the throne and sent it spinning out of control. Lines of laser light filled the smoky chamber, burning and cutting, as Anubis kept his finger on the firing button. Carroll levelled his launcher again then for no apparent reason found himself falling. A second later the familiar smell of charred flesh reached his nostrils. He glanced up and saw the Clown leaping towards the gyrating throne, then he looked down with dread to see, as he had feared, that his legs were no longer attached to his body. It was fortunate that unconsciousness through blood-loss and shock reached him before the pain.

♠♠♠

With that familiar metallic taste in his mouth Carroll wondered at the strangeness of thing – about how he had come to know both sides of death. He had killed. He had died. And he had seen things strange and terrible, and was now hoping that perhaps some degree of normality might now return to his life, or rather, familiarity, for his life had never been normal. He opened his eyes to gaze up into star-pinned space and knew that he was not in a resurrection machine. He could feel a hard floor against his back, the sensation of movement, wind gusting in his face.

'You wake,' came the Clown's voice in his mind, where he now realized it had always been.

'I certainly do,' said Carroll as he sat upright. He was on the back of the leaf craft, whilst the Clown, *the creature*, was at the other end of the craft guiding it away from the bloody eye of the sun. Carroll shuddered and averted his eyes, ostensibly to inspect his legs.

He was wearing the same clothes as before. His trousers had been repaired in some way, and when he pulled them down he saw that the same applied to his legs. There were neat scars encircling them just below his genitals. His arm had been healed also. There was no pain anywhere, no loss of mobility, only scars.

'Neat job,' he said.

The Clown's strange, blackly silhouetted head turned towards him. 'It is easier to repair than rebuild totally.'

'I didn't die then?' said Carroll.

'What is death?' countered the Clown, and turned away.

Carroll found he had no answer to that and turned to inspect the obvious alterations to the craft. All his additions had be removed and replaced by artefacts of the Clown's alien technology, some of which looked like living things, some of which defied comparison. The only things Carroll had any idea about looked like pedestal mounted road drills, which he assumed to be weapons of some kind.

'Where are we going?' he eventually asked.

'To finish the battle. To end the war,' replied the Clown.

'It is not over then?'

'No, the Four will resurrect themselves as did the Reaper, and will continue to do so until their source of power is destroyed.'

'And where is that source?'

'Under the matter converter. Under your steel plain, hence their swift reaction when I caused it to be moved.'

'But how are you–' began Carroll, but the Clown interrupted him.

'Now!' The voice in Carroll's head held menace. 'Now I have control again they will not trap me. They are done. Their time is ended.'

Carroll nodded, the skin on his back crawling, as something inside him shrieked, 'Alien! Alien! Alien!'

In time the titanic matter converter came into view and the Clown brought the craft to a mid-air halt. Carroll flinched as the alien reached back, but it was only groping for the veined sphere next to Carroll's legs. It picked this up and held it up before its. Immediately the sphere began to throb yellow light picking out the veins on its surface like rivulets of molten metal.

'Curiouser and curiouser,' said Carroll to himself, feeling he should have said it long ago. No cards here but discs, and the Clown certainly wasn't a white rabbit – a Jabberwock perhaps, but one no vorpal sword could slay.

Down below the matter converter shifted, changed its position like a giant in unquiet slumber, yet, such was its immensity, it gave the illusion that all else was shifting. Then, with the stately grace of something titanic moving, it rose. Carroll felt a tremor run through the air as it detached itself from the ground, then a low bone-numbing vibration as it went up and up. *An island in the sky*, thought Carroll, and repressed what he felt to be a dangerously uncontrolled laugh. A seemingly endless cliff of metal slid past. Carroll gripped the edge of the raft even though he knew it was an illusion that they were falling. He just could not make himself grasp on a visceral level that it was the converter rising, and they, so small and insignificant in comparison, were stationary. He only released the edge of the raft once the steel cliff finally passed and the whole huge object continued to rise.

At a height that must have been over five miles, the converter halted its ascent and began to turn over. It was then that Carroll saw its shape and, of course, it was hexagonal. He also saw something falling from it like dust from a table top. Ash? Mirrored buildings? Weapons? People? Carroll felt tears well in his eyes, yet they were not tears of grief. It was as if his body was frantically searching for a suitable emotional response to something beyond it compass. Perhaps next would come laughter, or madness.

Soon the converter exposed its top side to him and he saw the multihued glimmer of what he had known as the game-board. Then, as if some god had flicked on a light switch in fantastic heaven, the game-board flared with power, and rainbow light stabbed down at the plain below. Carroll shielded his eyes for a moment, then lowered his arm as fascination drew his gaze back. Below the matter converter lay a hole miles in diameter and descending into darkness.

'They made their base in this duct which leads to the main storage tanks of the disc,' came the Clown's thought. 'It is from here that the sea rises.' And as Carroll assimilated those words there came a roar as of titans. For a moment he thought he saw four black shapes rising from the hole, but in that moment they were erased by a vertical explosion of cubic miles of water. Carroll shook his head. This left him in doubt as to who was master here now. The time of the Four had certainly ended.

At length the light from the converter went out over the tsunamis below. As shock waves and spray crashed around the craft the gigantic shape of the converter began to move again. Mostly in silhouette it seemed to suck away the stars like some vast maw then spit them out behind. It made no noise now that its first piece of work was done.

'The seas first,' came the Clown's introspective thought, 'from them came the first life on your world.'

'How long will it take now?' Carroll asked, repressing the urge to ask if it would take seven days and seven nights with the usual rest period.

'The mass for the seas is stored within the disc. It will take one Earth year to bring it all to the surface.'

113

'Will it flood all the surface?' asked Carroll numbly.

'No, there are hollows in the disc to be filled up. We are in one now. Many large oceans are required here for balancing and cooling. They can be pumped to different areas of the disc should there be any precession or major heating stresses...'

'Then what?'

'Then land. Two years, perhaps more. It will take time to sculpt mountains and deserts and the like.'

'Deserts?'

'Yes... and for the enjoyment of the life I will bring into being here, the matter converters will themselves be converted into fusion furnaces – miniature suns.'

Carroll could not keep the wonderment from his voice as he asked his next question. 'And life... how long?'

'Another hundred years,' the Clown replied, swivelling its terrifying head towards him, 'already there are planktons and algae in this ocean. The matter converter did not merely bring the water to the surface. A less complex mechanism could have done that. In a year all the oceans will be in place and shoaling with life, but it will take longer to establish the larger fauna and flora whose information I have stored.' The head tilted then in what might have been introspection. 'Perhaps a decade or so after that will see all checks and inspection completed, then it will be time to resurrect the human race.'

Carroll swallowed dryly and licked at his salty lips. Nearby lay his bag, and in it the discs of his friends. A hundred years, he thought. In that time he knew he would see wonders. And it was little enough time to wait for eternity.

THE END

Made in the USA
Monee, IL
27 September 2023

43558474R00067